Tales from the Dragon's Cave

Peacemaking Stories for Everyone

**Written and Illustrated by
Arlene Williams**

**The Waking Light Press
Sparks, Nevada**

For Jason and Tasha—
As we learn, together, to create peace in the dragon's cave.
A.W.

Printed in the United States of America
on recycled, acid-free paper
using soy ink

Publisher's Cataloging in Publication
(Prepared by Quality Books Inc.)

Williams, Arlene.
    Tales from the dragon's cave : peacemaking stories for everyone
/ by Arlene Williams.
    p. cm.
    SUMMARY: Twelve original fairy tales, each depicting an aspect
of the art of conflict resolution for children.
    Preassigned LCCN: 95-61738.
    ISBN 0-9605444-5-3 (hardcover), 0-9605444-7-x (paper)

    I. Title.

PZ7.W655856Tal 1996   [Fic]
                                 QB195-20584

The Waking Light Press
P. O. Box 1329, Sparks, Nevada 89432

A Note from the Dragon's Cave

Below my house, dug deep into the earth, is the place where I write—my cave. It looks like a brightly lit office filled with books and cabinets and colorful pictures on the wall. And yet, in the far corner above the glare of the lights, I see a place where stalactites are beginning to form. I watch them become longer and longer, like golden icicles, as the lights grow dim and flicker out. Then, surrounded by darkness, I sense the whole room becoming a cavern, filled with crystals and columns and pools of deep water... and I become the dragon.

I am a wise and ancient dragon with many stories to tell. They were told to me long, long ago when people and dragons and other creatures of magic still spoke to one another. And though the stories here, within this book, are filled with conflict, they are not tales of dark evils and deadly battles. They are instead tales filled with hope, teaching us that those unending troubles which brew between ourselves, day to day, can have a brighter outcome than some might imagine.

Now a dragon knows, better than most, that conflict can ruin your life. There once was a time when dragons roamed freely everywhere. Yet, today, after battles with humans took a dreadful toll on our numbers, dragons can only survive in the darkest corners of the world like this writer's cave.

However, dragons also know that conflict itself is neither good nor bad—it simply **is**. There will always be problems in life, but the approach to solving these problems can be constructive or destructive. Many choose the violent way. And with that choice the conflict always grows.

Yet there are ways to solve our problems that challenge **us** to grow instead of the conflict. Those ways are wise ways that look within ourselves for the roots that conflict feeds upon. And those ways are the ones within my stories.

Listen carefully to these tales from the dragon's cave and learn from the many dragons you will meet. Some of them, you will find, fly. Some don't. Some breathe fire. Others have different abilities. However, none of them are dragons of the cruelest kind. The dragons in these tales have learned to step beyond the violent battles many still resort to. They, along with the other magical creatures in this book, want to show you solutions to your troubles that truly work toward peace.

So, listen carefully and hear a dragon's stories.

Table of Contents

Foreword

One of the greatest challenges in the field of conflict resolution is to make resolving problems, nonviolently, as exciting as violence. We are often numb to ever increasing violence. Young people are bored with anything less than fast-paced movies and video games chock full of random, and not so random, acts of violence. *Tales from the Dragon's Cave* offers a refreshing alternative—from the perspective of dragons who deal with very real problems.

I am honored to be asked to write the foreword to this wonderful new book of stories, particularly when I see the influence of the major themes of Children's Creative Response to Conflict so elegantly woven into contemporary fairy tales—affirmation or building self-esteem; communication skills, especially listening; cooperation, the value of friendship and working together; and finally win-win creative conflict resolution.

Arlene Williams masterfully weaves these four CCRC themes into four steps of Dragons' Peacemaking. In step one, we learn that dragons need to build self-esteem by building self-confidence—not by bullying or by putting others down, but by becoming confident in oneself and by becoming assertive not aggressive. We learn that dragons grow by learning to accept their mistakes.

Step two of dragon peacemaking involves good communication—learning to listen and to express feelings in a way that others can hear. The dragons use the Native American concept of a talking stick, here a "dragon stick", as a way of resolving angry conflicts. Only one dragon can talk at a time and dragons share how they are feeling. When dragons listen to each other, sometimes the conflicts are resolved just by listening.

Cooperation, in dragon language "the power of many", is the third peacemaking lesson for dragons. We hear how by working together we can often accomplish so much more than by competing individually.

The last path to peace for dragons is win-win creative conflict resolution which incorporates self-esteem, good communication and cooperation. All dragons can be winners when problem solving methods are used; defining the problem, brainstorming solutions and choosing solutions. All dragon skills are needed; good memories, the ability to concentrate and the ability to think fluently and generate lots of ideas. When dragons work together, win-win solutions can be found.

What an enjoyable way to visit or revisit our creative conflict resolution skills! Enjoy the dragons. Enjoy the journey.

Priscilla Prutzman
Co-founder—Children's Creative Response to Conflict
Co-author—*The Friendly Classroom for a Small Planet*

A Dragon's Path to Peace

Step One: The Highs and Lows of a Dragon's Esteem

There is a saying in the dragon kingdom: Dragons who make peace with themselves, make peace with the world. Indeed, examining the way you feel about yourself is the first step in the peacemaking process. The way you feel about yourself can be called self-esteem.

Self-esteem can be high or low, but it is not something you are born with, like your claws or scales or tail. It is something that develops as you grow—and it is something you can change.

High self-esteem means to think well of yourself. It does not mean feeling superior to other dragons. Dragons with high self-esteem like who they are. They don't mind the color of their spines or the curve of their wing, even if they're not quite perfect. They also have confidence in their own fire-breathing ability. They never worry whether their flame is longer or shorter than others. And dragons with high self-esteem find it easier to resolve conflicts with one another.

To have low self-esteem means to feel unworthy, or powerless over your life. Dragons with low self-esteem feel unhappy. Their cave is never big enough, their diamonds never bright enough, nor their flames hot enough. They may think they are ugly, useless or a failure and constantly tell themselves so. These dragons do not solve conflict in a healthy way. They either let themselves be pushed around or they become bullies and try to push others around. They may even run away from the world and hide from it, never venturing far from their cave.

However, like any dragon, you can raise your self-esteem by seeing yourself more positively. If you've always hated your tail, practice loving it. If you've always been afraid to do a mid-air somersault, take lessons and learn how. If you can't forgive yourself for losing that treasure hunting contest, look around your cave and appreciate the treasure you already have.

Remember, my dragons, high self-esteem comes by changing attitudes and thoughts. It comes by treating yourself, and other dragons, with respect. It comes by learning from your mistakes and moving on to success. And to show you how, here are three tales from the dragon....

For Especially Eager Dragons:

1. Read the stories, then make a "Dragon Can" from an empty tin can that is decorated with cut out diamond shapes sprinkled with glitter. Whenever you stop yourself from giving up on a project or chore or your homework—by saying the words, "I can..."—put a pebble in the can. Whenever you say or think something positive about yourself, put a pebble in the can. Whenever you help someone else in the same way, put a pebble in the can. When its all filled up, do something really special, like have a dragon party! And remember, you'll be sparkling bright, just like a magic diamond!

2. Drop paint, from a dripping paintbrush, across a blank piece of paper. Let it dry, then study these splats and plops of paint. What do you see? Dragon eyes! Fairy wings! Warty toads! Now finish the picture, changing these "mistakes" into something silly or wonderful.

Of Dragons and Diamonds

Once upon a time, an ancient marble city stood among a forest of olive and oak. Its tall, white columns and lush green gardens reflected perfectly in the still water of its long, rectangular pools. It looked like a paradise, so peaceful and elegant, but it was not a happy place at all.

The city was filled with magnificent creatures called centaurs who had the head and arms of a human and the body of a horse. They were a proud and noble breed, who regarded themselves highly. However, they thought so much of themselves that they wouldn't do any work. That's why they needed the mully-pegs.

The mully-pegs were stocky creatures—half-goat and half-human. Because they worked extremely hard, the centaurs kept them in the city. And, because they thought so little of themselves, the mully-pegs would do anything the centaurs asked of them.

One little mully-peg was called Sienna. She was a small creature with brown furry legs and goat-like horns on her head. She had strong arms and a healthy, bronze complexion. Her human-like face was quite charming. However, Sienna never thought of herself as beautiful for she was a mully-peg.

Sienna lived in the city palace and her job was to tend to the wishes of a young royal centaur called Vera. The little mully-peg spent her days bathing and dressing and feeding the centaur child who was always ill. Since Vera's biggest wish was to be as lovely as her mother, Sienna also spent many hours brushing the centaur's hair in hopes it would become long and glossy. However, because she was so unhealthy, Vera's hair was brittle and would not grow.

"You're not doing it right," Vera scolded the mully-peg one day. "If you brushed it harder it would grow."

Yet, when Sienna brushed more vigorously, Vera cried out in a rage, "You're breaking my beautiful hair. You can't do anything right. You're a useless mully-peg!" Then the little centaur threw the brush out the window. Sienna heard it clank against the garden wall.

"Go find it," Vera said cruelly. "I'm sure you can't. And if you don't, I won't let you have your supper."

Sienna rushed out to the garden to look for the brush. She had already missed her breakfast. Vera had dumped it on the floor. So, with her stomach grumbling hungrily, Sienna searched the bushes for the golden brush. "Oh, dear," she kept telling herself. "I'm not going to find it."

Then, just as she was about to give up, a voice boomed over the wall at her, "My goodness! I haven't seen one of your kind in a thousand years."

12

Sienna looked up into the fearsome face of a strange and frightening creature who was peering over the wall. "What are you?" she asked anxiously.

"Don't you know?" the creature cried.

Sienna shook her head. "I don't know anything," she replied. "I'm a mully-peg."

"You most certainly aren't," scoffed the creature. He puffed out a tiny wisp of smoke and explained, "It's been many years since I passed this way—perhaps even more than a thousand—but I definitely know that you're a faun and I'm a dragon."

The little mully-peg bowed her head. "Oh, you must be mistaken," she said nervously. "Not that you're a dragon. Of course you are. But I'm not a faun. I'm just a mully-peg."

The dragon blew an orange flame from his nostrils in frustration. "Someone has convinced you of being a mully-peg, you mean. But I know you are a faun. You used to be so plentiful a thousand years ago. The forest was filled with music from your flutes. Where have you all gone?"

Sienna bobbed her head again. "There are more mully-pegs like me in the city," she explained. Then she looked quickly at the dragon to see if she had angered him. "I mean," she stammered, "there are more fauns."

"And what do you do in the city?" the dragon asked sadly. "Do you play your music there?"

"Oh, you must be mistaken," Sienna murmured. "We don't play any music. We work for the centaurs."

"I see," said the dragon slowly. "And what do the

centaurs do?"

"Oh, they…" Sienna searched for an answer. "They tell us what to do."

"Yes." The dragon nodded. "Now I do see… and something is terribly wrong." The dragon looked thoughtfully at Sienna, then asked, "What is it you can't find? You were searching for something."

"A golden brush," Sienna explained. "Vera threw it out the window, and I must find it or miss my supper."

"Look for it then," the dragon commanded.

"Oh, I did," Sienna mumbled. "But Vera was right. She said I wouldn't find it and I can't."

The dragon snorted a flame again. "Let her look for it herself! She's the one who threw it!"

Sienna looked in alarm at Vera's window, worried she would be caught talking with the dragon. "Oh, please dragon," she whispered, "don't let Vera hear you."

The dragon glared at Sienna for a moment, angry at being told what to do. Then he calmed himself, realizing that the faun was truly frightened, and said with a gleam in his eye, "No, you look for the brush, little faun. That would be better, but first I have a gift for you."

Sienna shook her head. "Not for me?"

"Yes," the dragon declared. "And it cannot be refused. It is a dragon's diamond. It is very powerful." Then the beast reached over the wall and dropped a stone from his terrifying claw into Sienna's hand.

"Is this a diamond?" Sienna whispered as she stared at the lumpy, dull stone.

"Yes," the dragon answered. "But it is only a rough

one. It is not beautiful yet. However, within this stone lies the brilliant light of a magnificent gem. The light must be released."

"How?" Sienna wondered.

"With a thought, a powerful thought—a thought of yours," the dragon announced.

"Not mine," Sienna stammered.

"Yes, yours," the dragon proclaimed. "And if you want to see the light of the diamond shine, then you must start telling yourself that you *can*."

"*Can* what?" Sienna mumbled.

"*Can* everything..." the dragon thundered. "*Can* think for yourself... *can* speak loudly... *can* do things well." The dragon winked and pointed at the bushes, adding, "*Can* find the things you seek."

"Oh." Sienna giggled. "Oh, I see."

"Now, I'm off," the dragon roared. "But I'll be back to hear you play."

"Play what?" Sienna wondered.

"The flute."

"Oh, I can't—" Sienna started to murmur.

"No, no, no." The dragon interrupted. "Believe that you *can*. Believe that you *will*. Believe that you *have already*...." Then he blew one quick flame from his nostrils and disappeared beyond the garden wall.

The little mully-peg stared at the spot above the wall where the dragon's face had been. She had never met anyone so incredible. It seemed like a dream. And yet, there in her hands she held the dusty, dull stone. She looked down at it, peering at its brownish crust, wishing to see its light. Then she remembered the brush and her hungry stomach and the words of the dragon.

"I *can* find the brush," she mumbled awkwardly. "I *can* find the brush," she repeated more boldly. "I *will* find the brush," she told herself firmly.

All at once, something startling happened. She looked into a bush and caught sight of the brush. At the same time she heard a soft *clink* in her hands. When she glanced down at the diamond, she realized a piece had fallen from it. There was one tiny, smooth surface cut into the rough edge. It didn't gleam with light, but it was clear and shiny instead of dull brown like the rest of the stone.

Sienna hid the dragon's stone in the sash of her short tunic and grabbed the brush. Rushing back to Vera's chambers, she burst into the room, waving it proudly. Vera glared at her and pointed to an earthen supper tray dumped on the floor.

"You took too long," Vera said coldly as she ate from her own platter, "so I had to punish you. Clean it up, now, or you'll miss breakfast too."

Sienna rushed to clean up the mess, holding back a flood of tears. Her stomach felt so hollow and her heart felt empty too. She longed for some kindness in her life—something more than angry words day after day.

Then she remembered the dragon and the magic diamond. "I *can* have my supper," she whispered to herself. "I *can* still have my supper," she whispered again. "I *will* have my supper," she told herself definitely. And then, from the folds of her sash, she heard the soft *clink* of the diamond.

Sienna smiled and carried the tray and platter, piled with her spoiled supper, back down the long corridors to the palace kitchen. She bowed her head before a tall, worried-looking mully-peg. "Vera dumped the platter tray again in an angry fit," Sienna explained. "Please, could I have another?"

"Did she not like it?" the cook asked anxiously.

"Don't worry," Sienna assured her. "She was angry at me."

The cook gave her another tray, piled high with food for Vera. Sienna accepted it calmly and walked back toward Vera's chambers. Then, in a hidden alcove along a corridor, Sienna stopped to eat her supper. She giggled as she ate some grapes from the platter, knowing Vera would be furious. While she ate, she stared in wonder at the dragon's stone. Now there were two smoothly polished cuts in the rock, one next to the other. Each had a different angle and each one shone slightly. Sienna vowed there would soon be more.

By the end of the next day, there were ten cuts in the magic stone. Sienna was very proud. She knew her confidence was growing and so was the hope that the dragon was right—that she truly was a faun.

Vera, however, was becoming suspicious. "Mully-peg," she said sternly, "you don't seem as meek as you should be. Must I punish you more?"

Sienna quivered at the cruelty in the centaur's voice. "No," she stammered with a bowed head.

"Then tell me how useless you are," Vera commanded.

"I am just a mully-peg," Sienna mumbled.

"And you are useless?"

"Yes, I'm useless."

"And you can't do anything right?"

"I can't do anything right," Sienna agreed slowly. It was hard to say those words. She didn't feel useless anymore and she found it hard to be convincing. She hoped Vera would soon stop.

To comfort herself, Sienna slipped her fingers into the folds of her sash to touch the dragon stone. To her dismay, though, she found all the smoothly polished cuts had disappeared. Now it only seemed like a dull lump of stone again. Sienna supposed, with her denial of herself, all the work she had done on the diamond had been lost.

"What are you hiding?" the centaur asked quickly as she watched Sienna's face. "Let me have it."

Sienna looked in alarm at Vera. "Nothing," she stammered. "Just a lump of stone."

"Let me have it," Vera demanded, convinced it was something precious.

Reluctantly, Sienna handed over the magic stone. Vera looked at it quickly and denounced it with a sniff. "A useless thing for a useless creature," she grumbled. She threw the diamond out the window.

Sienna watched the stone fly into the dark evening sky. Tears came to her eyes. Then, without showing her resolve to Vera, she told herself again and again, "I *can* find it. I *will* find it. I *can*."

And so, when Vera fell asleep that night, Sienna crept through her chamber door and down the palace

19

steps to the garden. Slowly and meticulously, she searched the grounds where she thought the diamond might have fallen. "I *can* find it," she told herself a thousand times. "I *will* find it."

As she searched, she thought of Vera. How could she ever release the diamond's magic light and not make the centaur suspicious again? "I need to be clever," she told herself. "I *can* be clever—I *will* be clever," she affirmed over and over. Yet, inside, she feared she would never be clever enough. A little voice in her head kept answering back, "I'm just a mully-peg." Finally, Sienna whispered aloud in the cool, dark air, "If I were a faun, like the dragon said, I could be clever."

"You are," boomed a voice from the garden wall, "both a faun and clever."

Sienna looked up with delight at the sound of the dragon's voice. She hurried over to the wall. "Oh, you've come back. I'm so glad."

The dragon nodded kindly and asked, "Have you released the magic light from the diamond?"

Sienna glanced at her feet, embarrassed.

"I see something's wrong," the dragon surmised carefully. "But, no, don't give up. Believe it will turn out right."

"Yes," Sienna agreed as she stood up boldly to face the dragon. "I won't give up. I've lost the diamond but I *can* find it."

"Very good!" The dragon clapped his claws together. "Now where's your flute? I've come back to hear you play."

"Oh, I have no flute, yet." Sienna chuckled. Then she looked the dragon straight in the eye. "But I *will* learn to make one," she said decisively. "And then I *will* learn to play."

"Excellent!" The dragon applauded. "Now where's that diamond?"

"Give me a moment," Sienna said confidently. "I know it's here somewhere." She searched the bushes and then walked slowly across the lawn. However, she could not find it. "I won't give up," she told herself. "Somehow, I *will* find it."

"Believe you already have," the dragon urged. "Believe it's in your hand."

Sienna looked into the palm of her hand. "Yes!" She nodded happily. "I can picture it there."

And then the moon rose over the roof of the palace. Sienna looked up into its bright light and gazed across the lawn. All at once she caught sight of something glimmering in the grass. She rushed to it and picked it up. It was the diamond.

Sienna drew in a deep breath. She expected the stone to be dull and lumpy, as it was when Vera threw it from her window. However, now the stone was smooth, except for one rough spot still needing to be cut. The rest was polished in little angled facets, numbering fifty or more. There was still no magic light within the stone, but the diamond reflected the moonlight in a lovely way. Sienna clutched it and ran to the wall. "It's almost done!" she exclaimed.

The dragon examined the stone in her hand. He

nodded with approval. "You've done a beautiful job," he announced. Then he looked straight at the little faun and said, "I see a wonderful light within, just waiting to shine out."

Sienna blushed and looked at her feet. She realized he wasn't talking about the diamond.

"One more powerful thought," the dragon urged, "and the magic will be complete. What should that thought be?"

Sienna stared at the dragon. Suddenly a thought flickered into her mind. She drew herself up straight and proclaimed proudly, "I *am* a faun. Yes, a clever, musical faun. I'm not a mully-peg at all. I have *always* been a faun." She nodded to herself with satisfaction as she heard the magic diamond go *clink*.

Trembling with feeling, she looked at the stone in her hand. She could see it now, complete, with every facet perfect as it caught the bright moonlight. Her eyes grew wide. The stone began to glow. Then, as the stone poured forth a brilliant light, she heard someone call her name.

"Sienna!" came Vera's cry from the window. "Sienna, where are you? Come back or I'll call the guards."

Sienna felt the diamond pulse in her hand. She looked at the dragon with the light of the stone dancing in her eyes. "I cannot stay here," she told him. "I cannot be a mully-peg again."

"Of course you can't," agreed the dragon as he reached a claw toward her. "Can you climb the wall?"

Sienna laughed. "Certainly," she teased him, "I'm a faun." Then she tucked the diamond into her sash and wedged her hoof into a crevice between the stones of the wall.

However, as she reached for the dragon's claw, she heard Vera call again. Sienna felt a pang of guilt rush through her. "She'll be helpless without me," she puffed. "And she's so very ill."

The dragon grabbed her hand and pulled her to the top of the wall. "Oh, let her do something for herself," he rumbled. "She'll probably feel much better if she does."

Sienna looked back at Vera, who was staring, now, at the dragon. Sienna waited for her angry shouts, but to the faun's surprise, Vera was silent. Sienna could never remember a time in her whole life when a centaur was speechless.

"Dragon," she said quickly. "You're right. Vera would feel much better if she did things for herself. Do you have another diamond?"

The dragon breathed out a long flame toward the silver moon. He winked at Sienna. "You are bold, my faun, but clever. Yes, I have another diamond." Then he looked toward the centaur and called, "Now you must do for yourself, Vera. Your mully-peg is gone. But I have a gift for you. It is a magic diamond and if you've the courage and the will, you can make it shine brighter than that moon in the sky."

"How?" Vera called. Sienna had never heard her voice so urgent before.

"No one can do it for you. You must do it by taking care of yourself," the dragon explained.

"I don't know how." Vera moaned.

"Then you must learn." He reached into his pouch and pulled out another rough diamond. "Catch this!" he told the centaur as he tossed it toward the window.

"I can't," she shouted frantically as she watched it arc through the air.

"No," the dragon thundered. "Believe you *can!*"

Sienna clapped with pleasure as she saw Vera reach out and catch the stone. She knew there was already one polished cut in its lumpy surface. Then, for the first time in her life, the little faun stared out into the dark wide world she had never known. "It looks so big," she whispered faintly. "At least for a mully-peg, it looks big."

Gently, the dragon helped her down off the wall. Sienna smiled and took out the diamond. She let its light flow into the darkness ahead of her, adding, "But I'm not a mully-peg, am I? I'm a faun."

The Master of the Marsh

Once, long ago, on the edge of a wide salt marsh, there lived a boy named Philippe. His father was a fisherman who, from sunrise to sunset, tended his nets far out at sea beyond the estuary. Philippe and his elder sisters Marie, Danielle and Yvonne stayed alone all day, salting fish and mending nets and keeping the house in order. Their mother had died years ago and their father had never remarried.

During the day when their father was gone, the eldest sister, Marie, was in charge. But if Marie went to the village to buy a sack of flour, she left Danielle to watch over the family. And if Danielle and Marie went together, Yvonne was the one given authority. Being the youngest, Philippe was never in charge and he was always angry about it.

It wasn't that his sisters were mean to Philippe, for they were not. However, they fussed over his clothes, scolded him when he got dirty and made him wash his hands for meals as if he were a baby. "Someday, Papa will leave *me* in charge," he threatened them. "Then you'll be sorry."

Usually, when he'd had enough, he would take a spade and pail and wander down to the marsh to hunt for clams and mussels and snails. There he would watch the gulls and mallards work the mud flats for worms. Then he would search for shyer birds, hiding in the marsh grass. And wherever he went he kept an eye out for the great herons of the marsh, standing proud in the water as if they ruled over everything they surveyed. Philippe called the tall, long-necked herons, "The masters of the marsh."

One morning, Marie and Danielle went to the village, leaving Yvonne and Philippe alone to mend the nets. Philippe didn't want to do nets. He was angry because he could never go to the village like his sisters, and so his knots were not tight and his mending was not good.

Yvonne scolded him harshly, "Why don't you pay attention? You're not mending that right! You'll have to do it over!" Then the stocky girl tore out all of Philippe's work.

Philippe mumbled under his breath as he watched the tide flow in from the sea. He knew she was right, but he didn't want to admit it. So he pouted and glared as the mud flats below the marsh became swallowed up by saltwater.

"One day," Philippe promised himself quietly, "I'll be the master, like the herons of the marsh, and then my sisters will do what I say."

All day long, Yvonne argued with him over the nets. He worked on them reluctantly, never doing them

right. Then as the time approached for Marie and Danielle to return, Philippe laid his net work down and picked up his pail and his spade.

"I'm going to hunt for crabs," he announced.

"Go ahead," Yvonne snapped back. "You're just a bother."

Philippe turned abruptly and walked down through the marsh toward a small wooden dock hidden in the cord grass. It was a secret place Philippe had discovered. When the tide was high he used the dock for fishing. When the tide was low, he sat on the edge and filled his head with dreams.

The tide was flowing out. Already he could see the mud at the base of the pilings. Philippe sat quietly on the dock and watched as a great heron, standing regally on stilted legs, looked for fish in the shallow water.

The heron's beak bobbed below the water to catch a fish. Then the tall, masterful bird looked Philippe's way. Philippe sat very still, not even blinking. He kept his blue eyes glued to the heron as the bird's golden eyes stared back. And what Philippe saw in those eyes were the things that he longed for—dignity and self-respect.

"Someday," Philippe whispered to the heron, "I shall be a master of my world, like you."

Then the heron broke the gaze. As the fog came drifting in, the bird moved through the cord grass beyond his sight. Philippe sighed as he watched the heron disappear, longing for another glance at the bird.

Then he heard a woman's voice calling through the mist, "Is someone there?"

"Hello?" Philippe called back.

"Could you help?" croaked the woman. "My boat is in the mud."

Philippe waded through the cord grass toward the voice. Soon he saw an old, bent woman standing beside a small dory. "I was digging clams," the woman explained. "The tide went out so fast. I didn't realize the water in this channel was getting shallow."

"Get in," Philippe urged her. "I'll push you free."

The old woman climbed into the dory and Philippe shoved with all his might to free it from the muddy bottom. Then he towed her out to deeper water. "Can you row yourself home?"

"Oh, yes, my son," the woman assured him. "My home is very near." Then she picked up the oars and looked at him with a penetrating eye. "Tell me, is there something you would like?"

"I would like?" asked Philippe.

"Yes," coaxed the woman, "you have been very helpful and I sense there is something that you want very much. Tell me what it is."

The woman's stare made him feel anxious. He looked down at his hands. "I would like," he confessed awkwardly, "to be a master."

"A master? A master of what?" the woman urged.

Philippe laughed nervously, not sure why he was telling the old woman this. Yet, somehow, he felt compelled to say, "I would like to be a master of my sisters."

"I see," said the woman as she put the oars in their locks. "That is an interesting wish." She looked around

29

them at the fog and winked. "I feel there's magic in this mist," she whispered hoarsely. "Do you?"

Philippe nodded vaguely. The woman grinned a toothless grin and rowed into the greyness surrounding them. The boy lost sight of her quickly. He listened for the creaking of the oars in their locks. Instead he heard the flap of a wing and the squawk of a heron, "Krakk, krahnkk!" Philippe strained to see the bird through the mist, but no tall, slim silhouette could be seen.

He made his way back to the dock and headed for home. When he arrived, Marie was chopping onions for soup and Danielle was making bread. Yvonne was lighting the fire in the stove so they could cook.

None said a word to him as he entered, and Philippe felt uneasy. He sat in the corner on a stool and took off his muddy shoes. Marie looked at them and the footprints they'd left on the floor. Then she turned back to her soup, silently.

"Aren't you going to say something about my shoes?" Philippe asked with frustration.

"Your shoes are muddy," Marie said and went back to her work.

"Aren't you going to ask why they're muddy?" he persisted.

"Why are they muddy?" Marie asked flatly.

"I met an old woman in a dory who'd been beached by the tide," he explained, but his sisters ignored him. He glared at them. "Look at me!" he commanded.

Instantly all three sisters turned to stare at him.

Philippe was startled. "Don't look so angry," he

stammered.

The sisters continued to stare at him, but now their faces held wide grins. They looked like puppets.

"Stop smiling!" Philippe blurted out, annoyed by the strange behavior of the girls.

All at once, his sisters' faces went blank. They stared without blinking.

"Stop staring!" Philippe shouted. "Go back to work!"

Quickly the girls resumed their tasks, leaving Philippe alone in the corner to sulk. He thought that they were playing a trick on him, to teach him a lesson, since he had not done any work all day. It wasn't till supper was cooked and on the table that Philippe realized there might be another explanation.

"That bread looks delicious," he said hungrily. "I could eat the whole loaf myself."

Danielle picked up the loaf and set it on his plate.

He looked at her, bewildered. "I didn't mean it," he assured her. "Just cut me one slice."

Danielle took the loaf back and cut a slice. Then she brought it to him and laid it on his plate.

"Could I have some soup?" he asked Marie.

Marie filled his bowl full, then stood beside him blankly.

Philippe sat down and began eating. His sisters watched silently. Philippe looked up with his mouth full and sputtered, "What is wrong? Must I tell you to eat too? Go ahead and eat!"

Instantly the girls sat down to eat. Philippe's mouth dropped open. He finally realized what the problem might be. "Stop!" he yelled.

The girls stopped eating.

"Go to sleep!" he demanded.

The girls fell asleep.

"Wake up and dance," he commanded.

The girls jumped up and danced around the room.

Philippe thought of the old woman in the dory. He smiled slowly. "I'm the master," he told himself incredulously. "Now they must do what I say."

So Philippe let them dance while he ate. Then he had them stop to catch their breath. "Now go outside and muddy your hands," he told them mischievously. "Then come back inside and eat."

All evening, Philippe toyed with his sisters as if they were marionettes on a string. Then he heard his father whistling along the trail. Philippe jumped into bed. "Now clean up quickly," he commanded. "And as for all that's happened today," he added cunningly, "never tell Papa. Act for him as you did before I was your master."

The next day Philippe had a glorious time being in charge of his sisters. He made Yvonne do all her net work twice. He made Danielle wear her clothes inside out. He made Marie take him to the village and buy him a sweet to eat. However, by late afternoon, he grew restless, so he went to the marsh to look for herons.

There was one great heron standing in the shallows. Philippe knew it was the very same bird he had seen yesterday. "Now I am a master like you," Philippe whispered to the heron.

However, the bird did not look back. Instead the

heron rose on wide, slow wings and flew the other way. Philippe frowned, disturbed that the bird had gone.

All week long Philippe toyed with his sisters, making them do the work of four instead of three. However, the satisfaction of being obeyed soon began to wear off. He spent more and more time at the marsh looking for the herons, but the herons were never there. Philippe grew deeply troubled.

There had never been a time, before this, when he couldn't find at least one heron in the marsh. He began to worry that they had been killed or scared away. At other times, though, he felt they were still there, unseen, wading through the cord grass. More than once, he was sure he heard one fly away.

One evening, as the mist came creeping in, Philippe searched the tidal flats for the herons. Soon the fog surrounded him, blocking his view of the marsh, so he walked to the dock to think. Deep inside he had a terrible feeling that the herons were avoiding him.

"What have I done?" he asked the tall, lush grass that rose before him. And then he searched his thoughts for a reason that the herons would stay away.

His thoughts kept coming back to that wonderful moment when he had stared into the great heron's eyes. He saw again the dignity in that gaze and felt deeply the bird's mastery and self-respect. And then he thought of this week with his sisters. Suddenly, he was horrified by his memory of himself. He had become bossy and cruel. He wasn't like the heron at all.

Just then, he heard a hoarse voice call out from the

33

tall grass, "Is anyone there?"

Philippe recognized the voice of the woman. "Yes, I'm here! And I need your help!" he called.

"What is wrong?" the woman asked as her oars creaked against their locks. The tide was up and Philippe could hear the sides of her dory being scuffed by the cord grass. However, he still couldn't see anyone through the mist.

Philippe didn't wait for her to appear. "I'm not a master," he shouted with disgust. "I'm just a bully."

Philippe heard the oars stop. "You don't want to be the master of your sisters anymore?" the woman questioned from somewhere in the grass.

Philippe shook his head. "No! I want to be a different kind of master. I don't want to be a bully. I want to be like the herons."

All at once, Philippe shivered. There was an eerie silence on the marsh. He heard no scuffing of the boat against the grass, no creaking oars, and no reply from the woman. It was as if she had suddenly disappeared.

Then, as the echoes of his words rang through his mind, he felt something moving on the wood behind him. Thinking it was the woman, come to help him, he turned around with a grin. However, the woman wasn't there. Instead he found the heron watching him with silent, golden eyes.

All at once, a powerful feeling flooded him. It was the stirring of his own strong will. He stretched himself tall and proud like the heron and then he whispered, "You're not a master of your world at all, are you?" He paused a moment and let the heron's dignified gaze flow through him. "You don't need to be," he continued softly. "You're the master of yourself."

On wide wings, the heron rose up above Philippe, skimming the boy's hair gently with long, stick-like legs. "Krakk, krahnkk," the bird called hoarsely as Philippe nodded goodbye.

"Krakk, krahnkk," the bird called again, long after disappearing into that magical mist.

Later, when Philippe returned to his house, he found his sisters waiting for him anxiously. They scolded him about his muddy shoes and his dirty hands. Philippe listened patiently. Then he took off his boots by the door like they had asked and went to the pump to wash his hands. He didn't feel angry at them at all. He felt a calmness deep inside.

"And don't wander through the marsh in the fog!" Marie prattled on as she served up some supper. "You might get lost."

"Dear Marie," he said with a sense of authority, "I'd never get lost in the marsh." He looked at her with a twinkle in his eye and added, "There's magic in its mist."

"What nonsense!" Marie scoffed.

Philippe just smiled. He didn't need to argue with his sister anymore. He sipped his gravy from his spoon, noting how delicious it was. And faraway, somewhere across the marsh, he heard the hoarse, rough call of a heron.

Dragon Bluff and Blunder

Long, long ago, a young girl and her father climbed a steep, rocky path to a cliff above the sea. Kimi quickly found an open spot among the other village children who had gathered there to fly their kites. In her hands she held her black and yellow dragon kite which jumped in the wind as if it were anxious to fly. It was the first kite she had ever made completely by herself. She was very proud of it, especially since her father had doubted she could make one at all.

Her father was a famous kite maker. He had warned her that a dragon kite would be too difficult for a child her age to build, but she had made one anyway for she wanted to build it, secretly, on her own. When her father helped her with a kite, she always stood by and watched while he made it and sometimes flew it, too. All her life, she had dreamed of flying a kite as fierce as a dragon. Now, this dragon kite was hers alone to fly the skies.

Kimi adjusted the bridle one more time, hoping to

36

find the perfect angle for the speed of the wind. Then she let go. It caught the offshore breeze as it rose up, up, up into the sky.

For a moment, Kimi was ecstatic to see her own black silk dragon, yellow-striped and long-tailed, against the blue of the sky. She looked at her father with pride in her heart, hoping he would praise her for her success.

He was squinting into the sun as he watched the silk kite fly. "You're not a success yet," he advised with a stiff frown. "Let's see if it can stay up."

Then, suddenly, the kite took a dive. Kimi watched in horror as it zig-zagged right and left beyond control. She struggled to guide it with the kite string, but it took another downward dive and crashed onto the rocks below.

She stared in shock as the black and yellow colors of her kite were washed by the waves out to sea. She was so miserable, at first, she didn't even hear the laughter of the children all around her. Their taunts, though, soon came rushing in. She winced, embarrassed by her failure. Abruptly, she turned to run away before her father could remind her that he had been right all along.

It was never her intention to run far, but one hill became another and then another. Every time she stopped to turn back, Kimi heard the laughter of the others in her mind. She couldn't bear to face them, or her father, for she felt such bitter shame. So she ran until the sky stopped her with its thunder and lightning and rain.

Kimi took refuge in an ancient stone temple whose walls were covered with vines. Inside she found it dark, but dry, so she curled up on a long, flat stone and fell asleep. When she woke, she opened her eyes to a brightness behind her. Looking around, she saw the brightness came from two glowing, yellow eyes.

The creature was long and black, with stripes of yellow around his eyes and a yellow stripe running down his tail. She stared, as though the beast reminded her of something. And then she knew what the creature was. She recognized the soft, swishing sound of silk as he moved. He was her dragon kite, come to life before her eyes.

The silk dragon fluttered along the floor, wagging his head and looking at the ground. Once or twice, he opened his mouth and let out a miserable groan. Then he mumbled to himself, "How could I? I should have been watching. Oh dear. Oh my."

Kimi rubbed her eyes to make sure she wasn't dreaming as the kite-dragon moaned on and on. Finally she couldn't stand the whining anymore. "Tell me please, dragon," she asked, "what is wrong?"

The dragon kite turned and stared at her. Then he cleared his throat and said rather hesitantly, "So you are awake. Ah… well… you are my captive now. You cannot steal the magic stone."

Kimi looked down at the stone she lay on. It was carved with the design of a kite. "Steal the stone?" she asked with a laugh. She knew she could not even move it.

"Yes, this is the Temple of Kites," the silk dragon explained, "and you must not steal its magic stone. It is very powerful for it rescued me from the sea and brought me to life." The kite-dragon shook himself nervously all along his length. Kimi could see wide gashes in the silk on his tail.

"Oh!" she cried. "You're torn!"

The dragon kite nodded mournfully. "That is why you must not take the stone! Without the stone the Guardian cannot fix me."

Kimi looked around her slowly. "The Guardian?" she asked

"The guardian spirit of this temple. He rescues broken kites, such as me, through the stone's magic. I promised him I would guard it while he went to find my maker. He said if I guarded the stone faithfully, he would fix me when he returned." The kite-dragon shook his head from side to side as he moaned, "And now look! Oh, what a mess I've made of it. I only shut my eyes for a moment—while the lightning flashed. Lightning is so terrible for a kite. But it kept on flashing and flashing and when it stopped… well, now, here you are. Oh, I've made a mess of it. That's what comes of a dragon kite who can't fly."

Kimi felt as miserable as the kite-dragon, knowing it was her fault the kite had fallen and broken in the sea. "Why is the Guardian looking for the one who made you?" she asked cautiously.

"To punish him, I would hope!" snorted the silk dragon indignantly. "I was made improperly and now I'm almost in pieces. That is why I can't guard the stone. I'm a broken mess."

Kimi looked around her nervously, wondering when the Guardian would return. She didn't want to meet a temple spirit and be punished. "You haven't made a mess of this," she told the kite. "I will go and I will not take the stone. The Guardian will never know."

"But I've made a terrible mistake. He might find out. He may see you as you leave." The kite-dragon writhed across the temple floor, his black silk tail thrashing angrily.

"It's just a mistake," Kimi assured him. "I'll go. It will be fine."

She stepped off the magic stone and headed for the temple door when, suddenly, the silk dragon surrounded her. "No, you mustn't go. I must keep you here. Then he'll know I was guarding the stone."

"I've given up the stone," said Kimi angrily. "Now let me go!"

The kite-dragon shook his head. "You are my proof I was doing my job properly. The Guardian will be proud of me. He will be sure to fix me."

"You've made a mistake. Don't make another one. Let me go and he'll never know," Kimi argued, but the kite-dragon would not let her free, so Kimi changed her strategy. "Besides, why wait for the Guardian when I can fix you?" she asked.

"You can fix me? How? How do you know about kites?" the silk dragon challenged her.

Kimi bit her lip anxiously. She did not want to admit to her kite that she was his maker and the cause of all his problems. So she raised her head high and answered with a bluff, "I am a famous kite maker. I can fix any kite and I do not even need a stone. Let me go so I can fix you."

The silk dragon hesitated. Then slowly he began to

unwind. Just as Kimi was about to step free, however, the temple door opened with a rusty *squeak!*

The kite-dragon quickly coiled back around her, calling, "Guardian! Look what I've done."

Into the room stepped a bent old man. He was dressed in a worn silk robe and seemed almost ordinary, except for a soft light that glowed around him. His eyes shimmered with that same spirit light. They looked wise and understanding. "I could not find your maker," he told the kite. Then he looked at Kimi with surprise. "Who is this?"

"A famous kite maker—come to steal your stone, I suspect," the kite-dragon assured him. "But I fought her gallantly and captured her."

"That's not true!" Kimi sputtered. She stamped her foot in protest at the silk dragon's bluff.

The kite-dragon just ignored her. "Now will you fix me?" he asked hopefully. "I've done all you said. I've guarded the stone faithfully."

The temple guardian smiled at the kite-dragon. "Yes, you've done well," he said, "but I cannot fix you. I could not find your maker. Without your maker here, the magic of the stone will not be able to mend you."

The silk dragon frowned a moment, then brightened. "Ah, but we have another kite maker. She said she can fix any kite... even without the magic stone!"

The Guardian looked squarely at Kimi. She squirmed under his bright gaze. "A famous kite maker?" he asked with a chuckle. "How can you be? You are so young."

41

Kimi lowered her voice so it would sound deeper, more like her father's. "I am young, but wise," she said. "I have made kites since the day I was born."

The Guardian shook his head. He didn't say anything for a long while. Kimi feared he had guessed her secret—that she was the one who had built the dragon kite so poorly. She waited to be punished.

Instead, he said, "I am honored to have a famous kite maker here to teach me how to work without the stone. Please, dragon, let her go so she can show me how."

The silk dragon uncurled from around Kimi. Kimi stared at the Guardian, blankly, not knowing what to do. Finally she announced, "I need tools to work."

"Please use mine," the Guardian said warmly, pointing to a box in the corner of the room. Kimi peered inside. She found paper and silk of every weight and color. There were also knives and glue, thread and string, as well as different lengths of bamboo.

Kimi smiled, remembering those months as she built her kite. It had been so exciting to start. The black and yellow silk had felt so thick and luxurious. She was sure it would make a strong and beautiful kite. Kimi looked over at the kite-dragon. Even though he was torn and broken, he still looked very beautiful.

"First I'll mend your cloth," Kimi announced as she pulled out some pieces of black and yellow silk and began to patch the kite. When she was through, she looked at the broken bamboo spine running down the middle of the dragon's head. "Another spine is needed," she said as she quickly replaced it with a new one from the box. The last

43

thing she checked was the bridle. She cut the old knotted one free and made a new one with fresh string.

"There." She nodded happily to the kite. "You're fixed."

However, when the Guardian came to inspect her work, he was not as confident as Kimi. "We shall see," he said, motioning for her to bring the kite to the ancient stone. "The magic will tell us. Now hold that dragon still."

Kimi held the kite gently as she stood upon the stone. All at once a wind sprang up around her. There, beneath the tall roof of the temple, the kite rose up on an invisible kite line of magic. Kimi watched, in wonder, as the beautiful dragon flew freely. For a moment, she believed that her kite would fly this time, but soon the kite-dragon crashed at her feet, moaning and writhing on the temple floor.

The Guardian sighed. "If only we had your maker, my kite friend, we could set you free."

Kimi looked at the Guardian. "Why do you need the kite's maker?"

"So she can find her mistakes and correct them," he answered.

"Will she be punished?" Kimi said recklessly, not realizing he had tricked her into giving herself away.

The Guardian smiled. "Why should anyone be punished for a simple mistake? Mistakes are very useful. They help us learn, if we are willing." Then he put a hand on her shoulder and winked. "Besides, I think she has already punished herself enough as it is."

Kimi fidgeted nervously as the temple guardian

stared at her. She looked toward her dragon kite, still writhing on the floor. She wanted to run away. "I...I don't know what you mean," she stammered.

"Aren't you the kite's maker?" the Guardian asked gently.

Kimi looked at her feet. It was hard to admit her mistake. "Yes," she answered faintly. She let out a long sigh.

"You?" the silk dragon grumbled with surprise. "You made me?"

Kimi looked up at him fondly, remembering the thrill of building him. He was still a beautiful kite, she reminded herself. She could take pride in that. Raising her chin, she answered proudly, "Yes, I made you." She paused a moment and then added, "Please know, I did my very best."

The Guardian nodded at her with silent approval and picked up the kite. "Come, my dragon, we have your maker," he said happily. "Now the magic will work. Now you will tell us how to make you fly."

"Me?" the kite sputtered.

"Yes," the Guardian assured him, "through the magic of the stone."

Then Kimi held her kite once more as she stepped upon the magic stone. This time the wind didn't spring up. Instead, the silk dragon spoke to her. "I know!" he shouted, "I know what is wrong! My tail is much too wide and the silk is too heavy. You must slim me down, cutting all the excess away. Check the balance on my head too. I'm a little light on the right. If you adjust the bridle, I won't

45

wobble anymore."

Kimi worked happily, trimming the long tail of the dragon so it wouldn't drag down the kite. Then, with the help of the Guardian, she adjusted the bridle so the kite would be steadier. At last, she stopped to gaze at him with admiration. "You are a strong and beautiful kite, again," she said, "now that we've learned our lesson."

"And what is that?" asked the Guardian curiously.

"Don't cover one mistake with another," Kimi answered wisely. "Things will only get worse."

"And don't worry about making mistakes to begin with," added the silk dragon with a strong, steady voice. Kimi was glad he had lost that nervous whine.

"Yes, mistakes are to be learned from," the Guardian said calmly. "It is then that we can fly free."

Suddenly, the wind from the stone sprang up again. The black silk dragon rose up on that invisible, magical line. He flew steady and strong in the soft breeze. Then he swooped low and circled around Kimi and the Guardian.

"I can fly!" he shouted. "I can fly!"

Kimi smiled proudly at her kite. "Don't stop!" she called. "Don't stop ever!" She opened the door to the temple and let the kite slip outside. Then she watched him, with great joy, as he soared above the tree tops, higher and higher. Finally, she could no longer see him in the evening sky.

"Will he ever come down?" she asked the Guardian anxiously.

"Do you want him to?" the Guardian asked back.

"No," she shook her head surely. "Never."

"Then he will fly free forever," the Guardian assured her with a smile. "Thanks to his maker."

That night, Kimi walked proudly into her home. She went to her father and waited calmly for the scolding her actions would bring. He just looked at her, silently, for a long while.

"Where have you been?" he finally asked.

"Learning to accept my mistakes," she answered respectfully.

"I see," said her father. "Then it has been a good day. Tomorrow, I will help you build another dragon kite."

"I am grateful for your offer," Kimi said with a bowed head. "But I wish to start from the beginning, with a simple kite."

Her father nodded thoughtfully. "And may I help you?" he asked slowly. "It has been so long since I've made a simple kite. But this time, I will watch and you will work. I would enjoy it."

Kimi smiled and answered simply, "I would too."

A Dragon's Path to Peace

Step Two:
Dragon Words

Many dragons do not realize that a simple choice of words can bring peace. Instead, they rumble and roar and shriek as they battle other dragons. There is very little talking. But, to solve conflicts without violence, you need to use words. What you say, how you say it and what you don't say are very important to peacemaking.

First, dragons must be willing to speak with each other, instead of fighting or running away. Would you be willing to speak to a dragon who had just stolen your most precious ruby ring? What if she were ten times your size with a razor-sharp tip on her tail? Perhaps you would not have the courage to speak. However, to create peace with any dragon, you need to choose to talk together. Even though it can seem difficult, because of your anger or fear, it is the only way.

Second, dragons must understand that how you say something is perhaps as important as what you say. Are you shouting or mumbling? (Dragons tend to shout.) Are you talking too fast or too fierce? (Dragons can be much too fierce.) Many times you are too angry or intimidated to settle a conflict right away. So take a break and rehearse what to say with some other dragon. That way, you can speak calmly and with confidence.

Third, dragons need to listen to one another. Listening tells the others in a conflict that you care what they think and feel and say. Yet how many times have you been so angry with a dragon that you have interrupted them before they could finish? And how many times did they interrupt you? Dragons can be terribly impatient when it comes to taking turns. That is why you must take the time to let another finish before you speak. If you are truly listening, it won't be hard.

Finally, one of the most important ideas for working through conflicts is to take responsibility for your actions and feelings, instead of blaming others for theirs. A dragon argument is one where every dragon points an accusing claw at the others. A dragon discussion, though, happens when all dragons have the opportunity to express their concerns.

In an argument, you might declare, "**You're** always

knocking over my stacks of gold and silver! **You** make me mad!" Words like these usually enrage the other dragon. In a discussion, however, you might say, "**I** don't like restacking my coins. **I** feel mad." In this situation, the clumsy dragon does not feel so threatened. There is room to talk further, understand each other, and negotiate.

Good communication is worth more than all the jewels in your cave. Without it, you might not be able to enjoy your treasure at all. Without it, you may be spending all your days in battle. So learn well, dragons, from my precious stories....

For Especially Eager Dragons:

1. Read the stories, then make your own dragon stick. Decorate it with jewels or feathers or shells. Do a circle talk with your family, classmates or friends, using the stick just like in the story. Discuss a conflict or plan an event. For a greater challenge, lose your turn, for one pass around the circle, each time you use a "You" statement instead of an "I" statement.

2. Create a dragon puppet from a long sock, buttons and felt. Whenever you might have trouble speaking up for yourself, practice first with your new dragon friend.

Fairy Talk

Long, long ago, in the misty glen behind Greene's Manor, there lived a swarm of tiny fairies. They had lived there for centuries, among the rocks and leaves and flowers, without anyone knowing of them—anyone, that is, except a young girl named Cynthia Greene.

Cynthia loved the fairies. They were tiny creatures about twice the size of a dragonfly with delicate, shimmering wings. They flew like a dragonfly too, hovering in the still air, then darting off furiously with some strong purpose keen on their mind. Cynthia never tired of watching them. They were her own special secret and she made a silent promise to herself never to tell.

Of course, Cynthia really had no one with whom to share her secret. She was a lonely girl who had no friends. Her parents were often gone and she rarely spoke to the other adults at the Manor. They cooked her meals, washed her clothes and tidied her room, acting all the time as if she were a lamp or a vase or some other thing. Even her tutor, who came twice a week to give her lessons, was a harsh, strict woman, not a friend.

There were only two children on the grounds of the Greene Estate, Emily and Ruthie. They were the daughters of the gardener and they were extremely polite to Cynthia because her father was Lord of the Manor. However, when Cynthia wanted to play, they seemed caught up in their own games and not interested in Cynthia's.

So, for a whole year, Cynthia went to the glen to spy on the fairies. Almost every day, she put on her cape and strolled casually through the narrow green valley watching for fairies from the corner of her eye. Sometimes she'd climb a tree and sit there for hours, waiting for fairies to fly through the leaves in their buzzy, swarmy way. And sometimes she'd kneel beside the brook, looking for those special sparkles on the water that meant fairies would float by. The only times she didn't go to the glen were the days she had her lessons or when rain came down so hard she knew the fairies would be curled up inside a flower fast asleep.

She never spoke to the fairies. She was content just to watch them. Yet over the course of the year, she heard enough of their conversations to learn a little bit of fairy business and all their names. There were seven fairies in the glen—Sunbeam, Dewdrop, Windfeather, Earth-pounder, Dreamseed, Leafsong and Blossom. They were all sisters who spent their days tending the greenery in the valley from the tiniest flower to the tallest tree. Each fairy had a special job to do such as opening the blossoms of a flower, or watering its roots, or bringing sunshine to its leaves. Then, when the sun went down, they spent much of the night singing and dancing and playing.

One day, as Cynthia watched the brook for sparkles, six fairies floated by, two by two. She was quite curious to know where the seventh fairy had gone, so she walked up the stream keeping a lookout from the corner of her eye.

Finally Cynthia found her. It was Earthpounder, a brown-skinned, tough-looking little fairy with very muscular arms. She was sitting on a rock by the brook, sniffling. Cynthia couldn't imagine a fairy looking sadder and she almost began to cry herself. Finally she had to ask, "Is there anything I can do?"

Earthpounder looked into the young girl's face, squinting as if the sun were in her eyes. "Who's that shouting so loud?"

Cynthia lowered her voice. "It's me, Cynthia Greene."

Earthpounder stared at her. "What are you?" she asked.

"Don't you know who I am?" Cynthia replied. She was very puzzled at the fairy's question.

"No." Earthpounder frowned.

"I am Cynthia. I'm the person that plays in the glen."

"A person?" Earthpounder questioned. "You mean a people?"

"Yes." Cynthia nodded her head.

The fairy looked at her blankly. "Oh, I don't believe in people," she replied. "They haven't been around for

centuries."

Cynthia dropped onto the soft bank of the brook beside the little fairy. "You don't believe in people? But we're everywhere. How can you miss us?"

"Nope. Never see them," Earthpounder replied.

"But you see me right now. If I'm not a person, what am I?"

The fairy studied her hard. "Well, you could be a rabbit with those big front teeth, but you have very little fur. Or you could be an eagle with those beady eyes, but you've no feathers. Maybe you're a giant lizard without a tail? But, no. You haven't any scales."

"Couldn't I just be what I said? A person?"

"Perhaps," said Earthpounder slowly. "Where's your wings?"

"People don't have wings."

"What a shame." Earthpounder turned away. "Goodbye."

"Wait!" Cynthia cried.

"Hush! Don't shout," the fairy scolded.

"I'm sorry," whispered Cynthia, "but you look so sad. Is there anything I can do?"

The fairy looked at her blankly. "I can't imagine a people doing anything helpful. No there's nothing you can do."

"Perhaps I could listen while you talk," suggested Cynthia. "A respectful ear for your troubles is always helpful."

All at once, Earthpounder broke into tears again. "That's just it. No one listens. They only talk. Oh, how fairies talk. They all jabber, jabber, jabber. I can hardly stand it. They never hear what I say. I might as well be talking to a people."

Cynthia grinned. "Well, you're doing that, that's for sure."

A smile flickered across Earthpounder's face. She looked up at Cynthia. "You're not so bad... as long as you don't shout."

"Thank you," said Cynthia with a bob of her head. "But could you explain, what is it you want to say that no one listens to?"

Earthpounder wiped a tear from her eye. "It's about tending the plants. In the past, we all worked together, seven at a time. Then yesterday Dreamseed suggested that we work two by two, so we wouldn't get in each other's way. It seemed a wonderful idea until we divided up. Sunbeam and Leafsong went off together. Dreamseed and Blossom did too. Then Dewdrop and Windfeather..." The fairy grew silent. Her lip trembled slightly.

"The two of them went off without you," Cynthia finished softly.

The little fairy nodded. "If I could only make them listen, we could work together again. But they go jabbering off without me. They don't understand how lonely it can be."

"Well, I don't know how to make them listen. But I do have one suggestion," Cynthia said slowly.

Earthpounder put her hands on her hips. "Speak up," she demanded.

"*I* could work with you."

The little fairy looked at the girl with disbelief. "Me work alongside a people?" Then she let out a very hearty laugh.

Cynthia blushed. "Would it be that frightfully awful?"

The fairy shook her head. "No. No. I was thinking about the others and what they would say. They would be shocked and that would be delightful."

Cynthia grinned. "So?" she asked hopefully.

"Let's get to work," Earthpounder answered in her direct way.

And that was how it began. Each free day, Cynthia donned one of her oldest dresses and set out toward the glen. Along the way she'd stop for a hoe or a spade from the gardener's shed. All day long she worked side by side with the little fairy, digging the ground and moving it here or there. That was Earthpounder's job—to nourish the plants with good rich earth.

As they worked, the two became good friends. Cynthia told the fairy about the world of people, while Earthpounder taught the girl many useful things. She learned how to check the leaves on the forest floor to make sure they were rotting on schedule. She learned how to fracture rocks in the best way so they could crumble during icy weather. And, most amazingly, she learned that the other fairies couldn't see her.

Quite often, Cynthia would notice them hiding in the bushes—seeing just a hint of pink or gold or blue. Earthpounder always ignored them, disgusted with their whispers and giggles. One day, though, Cynthia stepped on a twig, making it snap. Instantly the fairies flew away and Earthpounder laughed, long and deep, at her foolish sisters.

"Don't bother about them," explained Earthpounder. "They can't see you because they don't believe in you. But they can see the earth move and hear the twigs snap and, after the stories they've heard about people, they're afraid."

"What stories about people?" Cynthia asked.

"Oh, old tales about people's stupid ways. For thousands of years, people worked with the fairies in our glen. Then, it seemed, they stopped listening." Earth-pounder shivered. "They attacked the trees with something sharp and shiny and knocked many of them down. Yes, people are stupid and dangerous, that's why they were banished from our kingdom in the glen."

Cynthia's eyes grew wide. "Am I dangerous?" she wondered.

"No," Earthpounder answered thoughtfully, "I wouldn't call you dangerous."

"Thank you." Cynthia grinned gratefully. "I'm glad of that."

All afternoon the two transplanted earthworms into a rocky patch of soil to aerate the roots of a tree. Often Cynthia caught a glimpse of a fairy flitting through the air far away. Then she saw something else in the bushes. It was the red head of Ruthie, the gardener's daughter. Cynthia looked carefully from the corner of her eye. She saw Emily there too. "There's someone watching us," she whispered.

"I don't care," Earthpounder insisted. "Let them jabber. I have no use for silly fairies."

"They're not fairies," Cynthia cautioned. "They're people."

Earthpounder looked in the direction of the bushes. "Yes, I do see something. Yes, you're right. It's people."

"They're girls like me. I know them," Cynthia whispered.

"Well, come out you two," Earthpounder called. "If you want to work with us, come out."

"I don't think they hear you," Cynthia said slowly.

Earthpounder looked puzzled. "Don't hear me? Must I shout?"

"It's not that," Cynthia explained. "These girls can't see you, or hear you. They don't believe in fairies."

Earthpounder glared at the girls. "Don't believe in fairies? Why not?"

"To people, you're just stories from long ago."

Earthpounder frowned for the longest time. Finally she laughed. "It's mad, it is. All these years, people and fairies have been ignoring each other. We've been absolutely ridiculous." She turned and looked at Cynthia with new respect. "But how was it that you could see us all this time?"

"I guess," answered Cynthia, "I wanted to believe in you, because... because I was so lonely."

"Lonely? What about them?" Earthpounder asked of the girls in the bushes.

Cynthia shook her head. "They play together.

59

There's never room for three."

Just then, Emily called out, "Cynthia, who are you talking to? Are you all right?"

Cynthia stared at them through the bushes, then turned away.

"Aren't you going to answer?" asked Earthpounder.

Cynthia shook her head. "I'd rather not."

The fairy looked at Cynthia thoughtfully. Finally she glanced at the other girls and said, "I'm wondering if you and I aren't being a bit too stubborn."

Cynthia nodded slowly. "Perhaps we are."

"We're ignoring them," Earthpounder declared, "just like fairies and people have ignored each other for centuries." Right then, however, she saw Leafsong pop up from behind a fern and giggle. "Yes, we're ignoring them," Earthpounder grumbled, "but my sisters deserve it!"

Cynthia looked at the girls behind the bushes, adding angrily, "And so do Emily and Ruthie!"

That evening, though, as Cynthia walked home along the brook, she could hear the footsteps of the girls behind her, struggling to keep up. Finally she turned around and called, "Hurry then. I'll wait."

The two girls stumbled up to her, breathless. "Oh Cynthia," Emily gasped. "You walk so fast."

"Aren't you scared?" Ruthie shivered. "It's getting dark."

"No, I always walk alone in the twilight," Cynthia said smugly. Then she remembered what her fairy friend had said. "But I can see it would be different for you," she added more civilly.

60

"Why do you talk to yourself all day?" Emily wondered. "And what do you do?"

"So, you're curious?" Cynthia replied with satisfaction.

"Yes," Emily confessed. "We've been curious about you for days, ever since we saw you take the hoe from Father's shed. What on earth do you do?"

Cynthia didn't answer. Then as they came out into the Manor gardens she turned to the girls and said, "It's late now, but if you meet me here after breakfast, I'll tell you what I do."

The other girls nodded and gave her their promise. "We will," they called enthusiastically as Cynthia walked away.

The next morning it was quite late when Cynthia found Earthpounder sorting through some leaves. "You're here, at last," the fairy mumbled. "Lessons with your tutor today?"

"No," Cynthia admitted. "I met those girls. They wanted to know what I do here. They kept me talking for hours."

"Did you mention me?" Earthpounder asked.

"Not directly," Cynthia assured her. "I just showed them how to look for fairies. They think it's a game. They're playing it right now, back in the garden."

"Good for you," Earthpounder said. Then she showed Cynthia how to help her with the leaves.

When they were through, Earthpounder stared at the girl in an uneasy way. "I hope you won't mind," the fairy began, "I talked to my sisters about you."

"Did you speak with them, at last?"

Earthpounder nodded.

"Good for you," Cynthia teased. Then she grinned. "And I don't mind if they know about me."

"Well, they don't quite believe me," Earthpounder explained, "but they love the stories that I tell about people. It's amazing. They all stop talking and listen."

"It is a good feeling, isn't it?" Cynthia agreed.

"Sunbeam and Leafsong even asked me to work with them today. I told them some other time." Then Earthpounder studied her friend's face thoughtfully. "You wouldn't mind, would you?"

Cynthia looked at Earthpounder and shook her head. "No. In fact, I've promised Ruthie and Emily I would play with them tomorrow, too. But I hope we'll still be friends."

Earthpounder flew up to look Cynthia square in the eye. "I wouldn't trade your friendship for all the fairies in the glen."

"Nor I yours." Cynthia beamed.

"Then it's set." Earthpounder said as she bent down to pick up a thick lump of earth. "Now, come on. There's a hungry little sapling over there. We've got work to do. Let's get on with it."

When a Dragon Says No

Once, long ago, Jinka, the dragon, lay in the warm sunshine above his desolate, rocky gorge. He was a dragon pirate, and as he basked in the sun, he watched the slow, swirling river below for any travelers he might ambush. It was not even a year since he had claimed this canyon, but already his cave was filled with heaps of gold and silver. Any who traveled down the river on its lazy current were trapped by the steep walls of stone. They couldn't escape the dragon, so they gave in to his demands for money.

This particular morning, Jinka caught sight of one lone raft coming down the river laden with sacks of rice. A tall boy was the only one riding on it. "Oh, too easy!" Jinka crooned to himself as he stretched his wings for flying. Then the huge, golden dragon swooped down on the unsuspecting boy.

As Jinka's shadow overtook him, the dragon called out, "You may not pass. This is a dragon's river."

The boy looked up and ducked, falling back onto the sacks of rice. Jinka clicked his tongue and gnashed his

teeth, and settled on a rock to stretch his tail from one canyon wall to another.

The gleaming tail caught the raft and held it in midstream. Jinka repeated his warning, "You may not pass. This is my river."

However, the boy hid himself behind a stack of rice sacks. He did not acknowledge the dragon.

Jinka became angry. "Listen, boy," he warned in a booming voice. "When a dragon speaks you must listen."

Still the boy kept hidden.

"Do not hide. Come out and face me or I will overturn your raft," Jinka bellowed angrily.

It was only then that the tall, thin boy stepped out from behind the rice sacks. He stood before the dragon, trembling violently.

"That's better," said Jinka with satisfaction. "But, not listening will cost you double. I'll take ten coins please."

The boy stared at him wide-eyed.

"Did you not hear?" Jinka roared. "I'll charge you more then. Twenty coins or you cannot pass."

The boy turned out his pockets to show they were empty.

Jinka studied the boy. He was certainly coarse looking and poorly dressed. His clothes were patched and his hands were rough from labor. "You are a farm boy on the way to the city to sell your rice," Jinka surmised. "But you travel alone. Where is your father?"

The boy looked sadly at the dragon. "My father died three years ago."

"And they sent you down the river without money?

Haven't they heard of me?" Jinka puffed up his chest, indignant at the thought that he wasn't famous yet.

"We have no money, you see, and you were not here last time I came. I didn't know." The boy raised his arms in a limp gesture.

Jinka shook his golden head. "Still, I cannot let you pass so turn your craft around."

"But I must sell my rice. My sister needs a wedding feast," the boy protested weakly.

"Then," said the dragon wickedly, "you must find something else that pleases me as much as money, or I will dump you in the river with your rice."

"I am very handy with clay," the boy offered. "I can make you something from the clay along the shore."

"What?"Jinka asked cautiously.

"A clay jug?" the boy asked hopefully.

The dragon shook his head.

"A clay jar?" the boy asked.

The dragon shook his head again.

"A clay pipe?" the boy tried a third time.

The dragon raised his head high and shouted, "No!"

The boy winced and hid behind the rice sacks once again. Jinka rumbled with aggravation,"When a dragon says no, everyone listens." The dragon took his tail and curled it under the corner of the raft.

"I am listening," whimpered the boy.

"Then find something that pleases me," the dragon thundered ferociously.

So the boy went through a listing of all the things he could make for the dragon. Eventually he suggested a statue. "Have you ever had a sculpture of yourself before?"

"A sculpture of me? What an excellent idea," the dragon replied.

So the boy tied his raft to a stunted tree on the thin shoreline below the red-brown cliffs. He collected some clay from the bank of the river and set to work. As he worked, the dragon watched him curiously and asked him many questions.

"What is your name, boy?" Jinka asked.

"I am Ohan."

"Do you get good money for that rice?" the dragon wondered.

"Not if I sell it in my village," Ohan answered. "But when I make the trip to the city, I do much, much better."

The dragon smiled, thinking about how many coins he could demand from the boy next time. "Then on your return trip you will have a lot of money?"

Ohan frowned. "No." He shook his head sadly.

"Why not?" the dragon demanded.

Ohan sighed. "Because my uncle will take the money from me."

"Your uncle?" Jinka asked slowly.

Ohan looked up at the dragon. "Yes, I stay with my uncle in the city, but after the rice is sold, he borrows the money from me and never pays it back. My family does not know that the little I bring home is ten times less than what I make."

Jinka snorted indignantly. "Why do you give it to him?"

Ohan shrugged. "He demands it. He is my uncle. What can I do?"

"Say no!" the dragon said angrily.

"I do," Ohan moaned, "but he won't listen."

Jinka raised his head proudly. "When a dragon says, 'No!', everyone listens."

Ohan smiled at Jinka. "That would be wonderful, to be like a dragon."

"I'll teach you, then!" Jinka assured him. "Your uncle won't get your coins this time. Now watch." Jinka sucked in his breath and raised his head high. Then he let out an ear-splitting, "NO." Ohan cowered from the power of it.

"You try," Jinka urged.

"I couldn't," Ohan said meekly.

"You can't refuse me—the great Jinka. Now try!"

So Ohan sucked in his breath and raised his head high. However the only sound that escaped from him was a faint, "No." Jinka snorted in disgust.

"I'm no good," Ohan mumbled.

"You're right. I can see why your uncle gets your money," the dragon grumbled.

Still, Jinka would not give up. For a good hour he coached the boy on the art of dragonly power. At first he was motivated by his own desire to take the boy's money. Soon, though, it became a matter of pride. Jinka could not admit defeat. It was as if Jinka, himself, was being challenged by the boy's uncle.

Finally Ohan collapsed on the river bank. "I'm not a dragon. It's no use. It won't work for me."

"That's true." Jinka nodded. "You're so young and small. You could never be like a dragon." Jinka thought for a moment, then added, "But perhaps you will not have to be."

"Really?" asked Ohan hopefully.

Jinka grinned a wicked grin. "Pretend to be your uncle. Demand some money of me. I will show you what to say."

Ohan smiled, then cleared his throat. "Ohan," he said in a husky voice, "I need a little money for a debt. I'll pay you back tomorrow."

"No," Jinka said sternly. "I cannot lend you money, Uncle, and if you ask one more time, I'll eat you with these teeth." Jinka gnashed his teeth threateningly.

Ohan stared at Jinka blankly. Then he burst into laughter.

Jinka became indignant. "How dare you laugh at me?"

The boy stopped laughing instantly, worried he had offended the dragon. He bowed reverently. "I'm sorry, dear dragon, but look at my teeth. I could never eat my uncle with them." Ohan opened his mouth to show the dragon a set of human teeth.

"Yes, yes," Jinka said quickly. "Let me try again." Jinka thought for a moment before continuing, "No, Uncle, I cannot lend you money, and if you ask again I will rip you with my claws." He nodded at Ohan with pleasure, then noticed Ohan's hands as they shaped the clay. "No, that won't do, you don't have claws."

Ohan nodded with amusement as he shaped the

tail of the dragon from a long rope of clay.

"I know!" Jinka declared. Then he snarled, "No, Uncle, I cannot lend you any money. Don't even ask or I'll smash you with my tail." But as soon as he had said it, Jinka laughed at himself, realizing Ohan had no tail either. "My goodness!" the dragon exclaimed. "No wonder your uncle walks all over you. You have no way to stop him."

"Precisely," Ohan said miserably.

"Now, now. Jinka never gives up. We must use our brains. Yes, strategy!" Jinka looked at Ohan and asked, "Why do you stay with your uncle?"

"I have no place else." Ohan shrugged.

"Surely, there must be another place in a city to rent, cheaper than all the money your uncle demands of you?" Jinka scoffed.

Ohan looked with delight at Jinka. "Yes, I never thought of that."

"And surely you could demand payment of all his debts, before he comes to your sister's wedding?"

"No, he is already invited," Ohan replied.

"But, but…" Jinka paused a moment to collect his thoughts. "If there is no money, there is no wedding, right? Would he not be ashamed to be the cause of that?"

"Perhaps," Ohan answered slowly.

"It will take a careful delivery to make him listen. You have no tail. You have no claws. You have no dragon teeth. But you can carry within you a dragon's confidence. And all it will take is practice."

All morning, Jinka made Ohan practice. First they decided which words would be best. Then Ohan said them again and again for confidence.

"Look me in the eye," Jinka advised the boy. "Not with anger, but with pride."

"Slow down," Jinka cautioned later. "Keep your voice steady."

"Not too loud," Jinka urged one more time. "You'll sound calmer and in control."

"No, that's too soft," Jinka corrected. "He'll never believe you mean it."

At last, Ohan gave his speech for the last time. "No, Uncle," Ohan said, "I cannot lend you money, and if you ask again I will leave immediately. I have come to be repaid for your past debt to me and my family. Without the money there can be no wedding feast. Do you wish to be the cause of that?"

Jinka nodded with satisfaction. "Perfect," he said. "I couldn't have said it better myself."

Ohan bowed, then he lifted up the sculpture for the dragon to see. The dragon beamed proudly. "What an exquisite creature I am."

"I'm glad you're pleased," Ohan replied with relief. He set the sculpture on a high ledge with strict instructions for Jinka not to touch it till it was thoroughly dry. Then Ohan untied his raft and sailed down the gorge, free of the dragon.

A whole week passed and the boy did not return. Jinka was beside himself with curiosity. He didn't even ambush any travelers on his river. He kept pacing back and forth along the cliff tops, peering down the river as far as he could see.

71

Finally, Jinka noticed a craft much like Ohan's heading up the river. Because of the current, it was being towed by someone walking along the narrow riverbank. The dragon crept to the edge of the gorge and waited impatiently. When it was clear to Jinka that it was indeed Ohan, the dragon swooped down on the boy immediately.

"Did you get the money?" he asked.

Ohan stopped and tied the tow rope to a tree. His smile was wide and his eyes were bright. He jingled his pockets. They were filled with coins.

"Did you say the words we practiced?" Jinka asked anxiously.

"I did!"

"Did you find another place to stay?"

"I did." Ohan assured him. "But I didn't need to leave. My uncle begged me to stay."

"And did he demand money?"

"He began to several times." Ohan smiled as he spoke. "But I just looked at him calmly, with a dragon's confidence. He never could finish."

Jinka sighed with satisfaction. Then he eyed Ohan's pockets. "Perhaps we should settle our little debt?"

"What debt?" Ohan asked casually.

"Twenty coins, wasn't it?" Jinka said smugly.

"No, dear dragon," Ohan answered with assurance. "My sculpture settled the debt. You know that I owe you nothing."

"Still, I could smash you with my tail," Jinka threatened.

"You could," said Ohan confidently, "but then you

would never receive an invitation to my sister's wedding feast. I thought you should be the guest of honor."

Jinka fell into the river with a splash. He was almost speechless. He did manage to sputter, "The guest of honor?"

"Yes, the guest of honor." Ohan laughed. "I know what a dragon likes. You've taught me too well."

Jinka blinked at the boy. Then he burst into a deep, husky dragon chuckle. "Oh, Ohan, my friend. You are so very right. I've taught you too well."

Ohan winked and reached into a lumpy rice sack. "Yes, I know what a dragon likes. Look. I brought you this..." the boy said merrily as he pulled out a large dragon shaped from clay.

Jinka clapped his claws with delight. "Oh!" he crooned happily. "Just what I need—another sculpture of Jinka, the dragon."

The Dragon Stick

There was once a green-scaled, long-tailed mother dragon who laid seven large eggs on a hot desert dune. When she was done, she carefully covered them with a deep layer of sand to keep them warm at night and cool during the day. Then she curled up to sleep beside the nest, guarding it until the eggs could hatch.

Not all of them did—as it often happens with dragon's eggs. One evening, as the scorching sun set behind the dune, four little dragons emerged from the sand. The mother licked their faces to welcome them and then set about teaching them to hunt in the desert night.

The dragons were clever even though they were young. One by one they stalked their meal, testing the air with their serpent-like tongues for the scent of their prey. Then, as they gathered the lizards and mice and snakes they had found into a pile, the mother dragon seared them gently with her flame.

It was the first meal the little ones had ever eaten, so all four dove into the pile fighting for their food. "No!

74

No!" said the mother dragon firmly. "You must learn to be dragon-like in my family."

Night after night, the wise dragon mother taught them well a dragon's ways. To do this she used a jeweled stick which hung on a chain around her neck. She called it the Dragon Stick and she would pass it among the little dragons whenever they had an argument. Only the dragon who held the stick was allowed to speak and so, being forced to listen to one another, it wasn't long till the young dragons learned to share and to discuss their differences in a respectful way.

When the argument was settled, the little dragons would curl up beside their mother to listen to stories of famous dragons and the world of people beyond the dune. Some people, their mother assured them, were friends. But some, she warned, were not.

And so, with their mother's loving care, the happy family of dragons grew quickly. Consequently, it was not long till the little dragons began to fly and to flame. One by one the great dragon sadly, yet proudly, sent them off into the world with their new-found fire and a special name. However, before the fourth one left, the mother fell sick with dragon fever.

"You will be my last," she whispered as the little she-dragon came close beside her and tried to warm her with a tiny flame. "And so I will call you by a special name, my own."

"Am I to be called Mother?" the young dragon asked with surprise.

The mother dragon chuckled softly. "No. I have

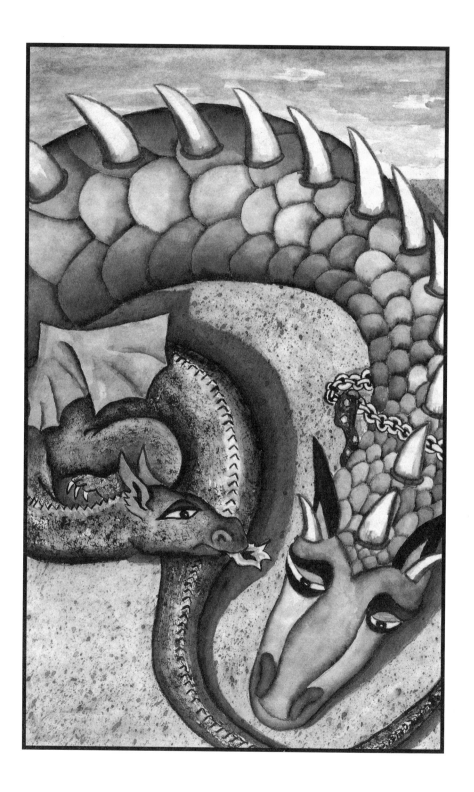

another name. I am called Wisdom."

The little dragon smiled. "I am glad to have your name."

"Also you must have this," the mother said as she pointed to the jeweled stick hanging around her neck. "The Dragon Stick was given to me by my mother. It carries the wisdom of one generation to the next."

"Is it magic?" the little dragon asked breathlessly.

The elder Wisdom took the chain from around her neck and put it on the little dragon's. "There is some magic," she said weakly, "but use it sparingly. The real power of this stick is the peace it has brought to many a dragon family. If you use it wisely, you can do the same." Then the great mother dragon closed her eyes and laid her head against the dune.

All night long, the little dragon breathed fire to warm her mother as she called out her name. Finally, when it was clear that the elder Wisdom would never wake again, the young one spread her wings to fly.

First, though, with an ache in her heart, she turned toward the silent, ancient dragon. "I will be a credit to your name," she whispered. "I will be very wise." Then she soared above the rising sun and headed east.

However, alone in the world, Wisdom did not feel wise like her mother. She felt afraid and kept well away from humans, not knowing which one could be trusted as a friend. All day she flew beneath the hot desert sun. Then, that night, she hunted mice, roasting them with her flame. Alone and in silence, she ate her meal and curled up to sleep in a deep crevice of an empty cave.

The next day Wisdom came to a small town in the desert. She circled high above it, wondering if these humans welcomed dragons or despised them. Deciding there was no way to tell, she was about to fly on when she heard a strange, but beautiful, noise coming from a large crowd in the village. She listened carefully, searching in her mind through all the stories her mother had told her about people. Then all at once she realized what the noise must be—music.

Wisdom couldn't resist. She circled lower and lower, listening to the pleasant sound. Her mother had often spoken with approval of human music, but Wisdom had no idea until now how wonderful it could be. It filled her head and heart and spirit. For a moment, she forgot how lonesome her day had been. Suddenly, she began spinning and diving as she flew through the sky, spell-bound by the melody.

Moments later, she landed on a rooftop. She hadn't planned to land at all, but she had pulled out of a dive too late. So, with a heavy thud, Wisdom crashed onto a large roof of clay tiles, right next to the crowd where the music was playing.

The music stopped. People stared at her. Some were shouting and pointing her way.

"Oh, goodness," the little dragon moaned as she looked at the crowd. "With a name like Wisdom, how could I be so foolish?"

Wisdom flapped her wings, desperately trying to take off. Tiles flew everywhere as her claws raked the roof. Ever so slightly, she rose in the air. However, she

78

could not fly away for there was a terrible pain in her right shoulder. At last she collapsed on the roof and let out a long weary flame.

The people below her screamed. Many ran. A storm of arrows came hurtling over the roof. Luckily, most of them bounced off her scales which were thick like armor. One of them, though, caught her in her softer underside. She moaned and let out another flame.

All at once she heard a voice below, "You are such a small dragon. How do you dare attack my village?"

Wisdom peered over the roof's edge at a balcony where a short, round man stood. She looked at him anxiously, for she had never spoken to a human before. "I didn't mean any harm," she blurted out.

"Then why did you attack?" the man demanded.

"I didn't attack. I fell. I was listening to the music and I crashed into the roof," she confessed miserably.

"I see," said the short man. He paced up and down the balcony for a moment then announced. "It will be excused, but as the Chief Elder of my village, I must now ask you to leave. You are on my roof."

The little dragon shook her head. "I hurt my wing," she explained. "I cannot leave. I cannot fly."

The man glared at her from under thick black eyebrows. "I see," he muttered. Then he paced up and down for a much longer time.

Suddenly, a woman appeared on the balcony. "Wyam! The children are fighting again! Come!" she pleaded.

"Not now, Sanda," he growled. "Can't you see

there's a dragon on the roof?"

"But Nolo has Rytt by the neck and Jenu has Zimmy against the wall," the woman protested.

The man let out an angry groan. "Nolo! Jenu!" he warned as he stormed off the balcony. "Stop that!"

Wisdom listened with her keen dragon ears as a flurry of accusations and threats were unleashed within the house. Everyone was talking at the same time. The little dragon just shook her head at the confusion and told herself, "People's ways are very different from those of dragons."

Finally the short, round man named Wyam came back. He was not in a good mood. He shook his finger at the dragon. "You must leave at once, even if you have to walk. I cannot let you scare my people with your flames."

"I would love to leave," Wisdom said sincerely, "but there's no way down from your roof."

The Chief Elder studied the roof. Finally he shrugged. "Yes, you are too big for the ladder, so you have permission to rest there three days. But if you use your flames against my people, you will be killed," the Elder said sternly. Then he commanded his bowmen to watch the dragon and marched abruptly back inside his house.

All day, Wisdom lay on the roof under the hot sun, listening to the endless arguments of the children in the Elder's house below her. Their fighting went on and on. None of them heard what the others said, and their voices were filled with blame. It was always someone else's fault so nothing was ever settled. Wisdom thought back to her own brothers and sisters as they learned to pass the

Dragon Stick. She was very glad she was a dragon.

Then, as the sun went down behind the rooftops, the Elder came out on his balcony looking very weary. He sat down on a bench and cupped his chin in his hand. "Oh, why did I ever have children?" he muttered.

Wisdom looked down. "Is something wrong?" she asked.

He shook his head. "Is something wrong? My children argue endlessly, that's what's wrong."

"Can't you teach them not to fight?" the dragon asked.

Wyam threw up his hands. "If someone could teach my children not to fight, I would give them anything."

"I could teach them," the dragon answered simply.

The man stared at her in amazement. Finally, he asked hopefully, "You could?"

Wisdom nodded proudly. "I am very wise. My name is Wisdom."

"And what would you ask for in payment?" he inquired slowly.

Wisdom looked at him thoughtfully. At last she answered, "I would ask for this arrow out of my side, some steps to get off this roof and some good fat mice to eat." She paused a moment, dreamily remembering the beautiful music she heard that morning. "And," she continued, "a place where I can always hear music."

"Is that all?" the Elder sputtered.

"Should I ask for more?" Wisdom wondered, concerned that she had done something improper.

"Oh, no!" Wyam shook his head. "That is enough."

"Good!" The dragon sighed with relief. "Now if one of your men could pull out this arrow and bring me some mice for a meal, I can make my plan."

That night, Wisdom lay beneath the stars eating her mice raw so she wouldn't scare the humans with her flame. She thought of her mother and sisters with great longing, remembering how easy it had been to settle arguments between them. "But these boys," she told herself, "they are full of anger. I must give them a reason to learn." She looked at the Dragon Stick, thinking of the magic and power that it held. She nodded to herself. "Yes, a very good reason."

Then, aching all over from her wound and her wing, the wise little dragon fell asleep.

The next morning, Wisdom called to the Elder. Soon, he appeared on the balcony. "You have a plan?" he asked hopefully.

"A very good plan," Wisdom assured him. "Please raise a ladder to the roof and bring me your sons the moment they start fighting."

"I will bring them to you," the man promised as he raised up a ladder. "Definitely."

It wasn't very long till Wisdom heard a loud, unruly argument coming from the Elder's house. Quickly she went to the edge of the roof. In a moment, the Elder appeared with four short, dark-haired boys who looked very much like their father.

She stared at the boys and announced forcefully, "I am a most patient dragon, especially because your father has let me be a guest on your roof. But I am afraid I cannot tolerate your quarreling any longer." She stopped a moment to send a long, orange flame above the heads of the boys. Then she raised her jewelled stick high into the air. "I am the keeper of the Dragon Stick," she advised them, "and with one sweep of this powerful magic, I can turn you all into mice."

The boys stared at her with their mouths as wide as canyons.

"However, knowing people are very bright creatures, I will give you each a chance to be spared. Which ones among you are worthy of that chance?"

All four boys raised their hands and waved them urgently.

"Fine then." Wisdom nodded. "Come up to the roof."

Soon all four boys sat before her in a circle. "We shall play a game, a dragon game, and if you succeed, I shall let you stay as boys. If you don't..." the dragon stared at each one fiercely, "then you shall be my dinner."

The boys sat up straight, listening intently.

"There is only one rule—you may speak only when you hold the stick. When you have the stick, no one may interrupt you. Then, when you're done, pass the stick to the next boy," Wisdom instructed them. "Now, who wants to be the first to discuss the fight?"

All four boys reached eagerly for the stick. Wisdom handed it to the boy nearest her. "You begin. What is your name?"

"My name is Zimmy," said the boy respectfully to the dragon. Then he turned to his brother, Rytt, and waved the stick. "Ha! I get to be first. You never let me be first. You're always so pushy."

Rytt grabbed the stick from Zimmy. "I'm not pushy, and if you'd stop calling me names, I'd let you be first."

With that, Nolo grabbed the stick. "And if you'd stop hitting everyone, Rytt, no one would call you names."

"I'm not the only one that hits," Rytt blurted out.

"Yes, you are," Zimmy insisted.

All at once, Jenu jumped up and took hold of the stick. "There, you're doing it again, all of you. You never listen to me. It's my turn and you won't listen."

And the next moment, no one was listening to anyone for the boys were all shouting at once.

"Be quiet!" Wisdom thundered as she breathed a flame of warning above each boy's head.

The boys were suddenly quiet. They stared toward the dragon fearfully. "Are you going to eat us?" Jenu stammered.

"I should," Wisdom declared angrily. "But I think you boys can learn if I give you one more chance." Then she paused a moment, thinking of her wise mother and wondering what she might do. Passing the stick, Wisdom realized, would do no good if the boys continued to blame and blame and blame.

Wisdom breathed another quick, short flame. "We need a new rule that will help you learn to play," she announced. "It should be... ah, yes!" She nodded with authority. "Listen carefully. When you have the stick you can only speak of yourself—how you feel. If you complain of what another's done you will have to leave the circle.

You will have failed. Do you agree?"

The boys stared blankly, not understanding.

Wisdom cleared her throat and began again, "Begin each sentence with the word 'I'. If you say 'you' or 'they' or your brother's name, you will lose the game." She held out the stick. "Who wants to be first?"

All four shook their head and shrank away from the stick.

"Then I'll choose," Wisdom said calmly. "Nolo you be first."

The dragon dropped the stick into Nolo's lap. He stared at it in horror, not saying a word.

Wisdom let a little smoky rumble escape from her throat. "That was my stomach," she warned him. "I'm getting hungry."

Quickly, Nolo picked up the stick. "Ah, I uh…" he stammered, struggling to keep to the rule. "I'm mad at… no, I'm mad because… no, I'm just mad."

The dragon nodded as Nolo passed the stick to Jenu.

"I'm mad too," Jenu said with a glare. He passed the stick to Rytt.

"Me too." Rytt nodded giving the stick to Zimmy.

"I'm very mad," Zimmy said defiantly. "I'm the maddest." Nolo reached for the stick but Zimmy kept hold of it. "I'm the maddest," Zimmy continued, "because… because I hate being last."

He handed the stick to Nolo who snatched it up. "I'm really the maddest," he said with a glare at Zimmy, "because I…I hate being hit."

He sat nodding to himself for a long moment. Finally he passed the stick to Jenu.

"I have to be the mad, mad, maddest," Jenu announced, "because I don't like being ignored." He threw the stick to Rytt angrily.

Rytt caught the stick and waved it wildly above his head. "The very, very, very maddest is me," he shouted, "I don't like to be called names." Then he stared at the other boys. "I don't want anyone to ever call me a name again."

Zimmy reached out for the stick. Rytt handed it to him. "I wish sometimes I could be first."

"And I wish I would never be hit," Nolo said when he was passed the stick. "I wish I would never be pinched. I wish I would never be scratched." He went on and on, wishing that he would never be pushed or poked or choked again. At last he offered the stick to Jenu.

Jenu stared at all his brothers. "And I wish what I say would be heard." Then he smiled a moment as he held the stick firmly in his hands. "Yes, it's nice to feel I am heard." All at once he laughed softly. "And I don't feel so mad anymore."

He passed the stick to Rytt. Rytt shrugged. "I don't either."

The stick went to Zimmy and to Nolo. Neither of them felt angry at all. They laid the stick at the center of the circle and looked at the dragon. "We're done," they all said with a grin.

Wisdom blew a little flame of approval. "Yes, I can see that you're done..." She winked at the boys. "Until the next fight."

And so, Wisdom let the boys back down the ladder after they had all firmly promised to call for the Dragon Stick whenever they argued. From that day on, the Elder's house grew very peaceful because the boys began to listen to each other and not to blame.

And the very next day, some carpenters came to build steps down from the rooftop. Slowly, the little dragon slithered down them to the balcony where she spent many pleasant days as a guest of the Elder, nursing her wing and the wound in her side. Every evening she ate delicious meals of roasted mice, which Wyam was only too happy to provide, while someone from the village serenaded her with music.

At last the wing healed and the wound in her soft underside disappeared. However, by then, Wisdom had grown so fond of Nolo and Jenu and Rytt and Zimmy, that she decided to settle there in the village. The Elder built her a cave-like home next to theirs, and Wisdom delighted everyone in the town by catching mice in the streets and alleyways.

Of course, Wisdom always wore the Dragon Stick proudly around her neck. She reminded the children of it often. And whenever any of them fought too much amongst themselves, their parents always brought them for a visit to the wise little dragon.

A Dragon's Path to Peace

Step Three: Dragons Can Cooperate!

Many a dragon knows that the best way to end a conflict is to agree to work together to solve the problem, instead of fighting over it. Working together is called cooperation. Some dragons call it—the power of many. No matter what it is called, it can have amazing results.

In order to cooperate, both sides must give up that struggle for power where there are winners and losers. Dragons are usually delighted to win an argument. You may find great pleasure in being right about that last line in an old dragon verse or proving you're the fastest in a flying race. However, you pay the price of having to struggle constantly with others who also want to win. This is the way enemies are created.

However, there is an alternative to living with enemies. That alternative is to see other dragons as part of a team. It only takes a change in attitude to accomplish this, yet this change can be very difficult for dragons to make.

Indeed, you may often choose to not work together, believing that your method for breaking a curse is best or that you don't need anyone's help to find a sunken treasure ship. Dragons are often swayed by a sense of their own power. Yet one dragon mind is much less powerful than two. By reaching out to solve problems together, you create a climate for peace to begin. And because every dragon has their own unique magic to contribute, the end result will be stronger than what could come from working alone.

Cooperation is an attitude. It is an attitude that creates peace. Treasure that attitude and share it generously—as generously as I share with you my stories....

For Especially Eager Dragons:

1. Read the stories and then play a game with your friends. Give everyone a piece of colored paper (use several colors) and have them cut out or tear out one shape. Don't tell them ahead of time what the shapes are for. When everyone is done, have the whole group arrange their shapes on a larger sheet to make a dragon. Decide as a group which shape should be the head, which should be the tail, etc. Glue them down and name your dragon. You can even write a story, together, about him or her!

2. Make a "Curiosity List". Pick someone you don't know well, and feel you could never like as a friend. List questions you could ask them that might help you know and understand them better. Get curious! Try really asking them the questions. Perhaps you'll turn a potential enemy into a friend.

Pixie Tuggles

Many magical years ago, on the broad plain of a savannah land, a child named Jessaya was born to a wealthy merchant family. She grew into a small, quick girl with wiry black hair and a willful spirit. Being the only child of the family, she was used to having her way, and when she didn't get what she wanted, her large, brown eyes flashed with anger.

One hot day in summer, Aunt Humiah and Cousin Bonoi came to visit from a port city in the north. After hugs and laughter and the giving of gifts, they sat down to eat beneath a large baobab tree beside the house. And as they ate, Aunt Humiah told them seafarers' tales of magical creatures from faraway places.

"Yes, there are many wonderful things one sees and hears of in the northland," Aunt Humiah said as the sun began to set. "And also some things which are not so wonderful."

"Like what?" Jessaya asked eagerly.

"Like rainbow pixies," Bonoi groaned.

"Rainbow pixies?" Jessaya repeated.

"Tiny little people who stow away on ships or sneak into your home at night." he explained. "They're from a land that is far, far away and they glow like the rainbow."

"You mean their skin isn't brown or black?" Jessaya whispered with wide eyes.

Bonoi shook his head. "Their colors swirl across their skin like the bands of the rainbow."

"Really?" Jessaya sighed. "I wish I could see one. Did you bring one along?"

"I hope not!" Aunt Humiah laughed. "And you wouldn't want one if we did."

"Why not?"

"Because there's always two of them, filled with mischief, and they tuggle endlessly," Aunt Humiah said with a smile.

"Tuggle?" Jessaya questioned.

"That means they fight," Bonoi grumbled, "all night long."

"Oh," Jessaya said slowly, still longing to see just what a rainbow pixie looked like.

Then Aunt Humiah asked Jessaya for a song. Bonoi jumped up to join her. "Let's sing the goat song," he suggested.

Jessaya nodded, and the two began. However, they found themselves each singing a different tune. "That's not how to sing it!" Jessaya shouted at her cousin.

"That's how *I* sing it," Bonoi argued.

"I want to sing it *my* way!" Jessaya commanded.

92

"No, I want to sing it *my* way!" Bonoi demanded.

"Let's not sing at all," Jessaya's father announced. "It's time to sleep."

And so, with a glaring good night, the cousins marched off to their rooms. Jessaya didn't sleep well, however. She tossed about, on her clay bed, still angry with her cousin. Her dreams were filled with voices that argued constantly. Finally she woke up and realized that those voices were right beside her.

Jessaya sat up on her sleeping mat and peered into the darkness. Instantly, she cried out with delight. Below her, she saw two little people who were definitely rainbow pixies. They shimmered green and yellow and blue and red.

She was so dazzled by the sight of them, that it took a moment for her to realize what they were fighting about. Then, all at once, she realized they each had hold of her sandal. One pixie was pulling one way and the second was pulling the other.

"Let's go *this* way," one was shouting.

"No *this* way," the other yelled back.

Jessaya giggled to herself. It was an amusing sight. Neither one would give in and so they just pulled and tugged, back and forth, never going anywhere with her sandal.

She watched them for most of an hour, then curled back up on her sleeping mat. She couldn't get to sleep, however, with the voices of the tiny pixies filling the darkness. So she just sighed and listened and laughed at the silly pixies till the sun came up.

The voices stopped suddenly. Sleepily, Jessaya looked beside her. The pixies were gone, but her sandal wasn't. She grinned and yawned, then closed her eyes and went to sleep.

It was almost noon when her mother shook her awake. "What's wrong Jessaya? Are you sick?"

"It was the pixies," Jessaya muttered. "The rainbow pixies."

Her mother looked around the room. "There are no pixies here. It must have been a dream. Now hurry and dress and eat. Bonoi is waiting to play."

Jessaya got up slowly, not anxious to see Bonoi again. She feared he would be as bossy as he was yesterday.

All day long, Bonoi and Jessaya fought. When they tried to play the stick game, they each had different rules. When they began to build a fort in the baobab tree, they each had a different plan. They didn't find anything on which they could agree. Even when Jessaya told Bonoi about the pixies, he accused her of lying for he insisted they hadn't brought any with them.

At last, tired and cranky, Jessaya tumbled onto her mat. She closed her eyes and fell into a deep, but disturbed sleep. It seemed just a moment later, when she woke up with a jump. And yet, she realized, it must be late in the night for the rainbow pixies were fighting over her sandal again.

"*This* way," one shouted.

"No let's go *this* way," the other yelled.

Jessaya peeked over the edge of the bed to see

their charming colors. Tonight, however, the shimmer of their rainbow light couldn't hold her attention for long. She noticed right away how shrill their voices seemed and how silly their argument was. This time she was determined to stop it.

"What are you trying to do?" she demanded of the pixies.

"We're trying to steal your shoe," one of them muttered.

Jessaya laughed. "When you steal something, you are supposed to be quiet."

"But *he* won't go the right way," said the second pixie.

"You mean *you* won't go the right way," protested the first.

Jessaya shook her head. "But you spend all your time fighting and you're getting nowhere. Why don't one of you just let go?" Jessaya suggested.

Both little pixies stared at her for a moment as if she had said the impossible. "I'll *never* let go!" the first one declared as he tugged even harder on the shoe.

"And neither will *I*," said the second who was tugging so hard all the bands of colors on his face turned bright red.

"Then I'll just take the sandal away from you," Jessaya declared. She reached over and grabbed the shoe. Instantly the rainbow pixies disappeared into the darkness, as if their colorful light had been blown out.

With a sigh, Jessaya tucked the shoe under her mat and closed her eyes to sleep. Immediately, she heard the pixies arguing again. This time they were arguing over her comb. Jessaya groaned and grabbed the comb. The pixies disappeared, but not for long. A minute later they were arguing over her bracelet.

All night long, Jessaya grumbled and growled as the two little pixies fought. Then, when dawn came, the fighting stopped and Jessaya drifted into sleep.

It was almost noon when her mother shook her awake. "What is wrong with you, Jessaya?" she asked with irritation.

Jessaya mumbled wearily, "Pixie tuggles."

"Pixie dreams, you mean," her mother said sternly. "It's Bonoi's last day here. Try to be nice."

However, this day started off like the last. When they tried to play hoop ball they each had a different way to throw. When they tried to dance the stork dance, they each had different steps. Finally Jessaya suggested, "Let's walk to the river. Perhaps there's something there we can both do."

The river was wide and slow. Together they watched hippos and zebras and wildebeests drink along its shores. And, together, they stalked storks and other birds in the high grass. Then they found a long flat log floating by the bank. "Let's go for a ride!" Bonoi cried.

They waded out to the log, forging through the water as if in a race. Bonoi climbed on one end, facing upstream. Jessaya climbed on the other, facing downstream.

"I'm the leader!" Jessaya declared with authority.

"No! I'm the leader!" Bonoi protested.

Then they both paddled with their hands as hard as they could in the direction that they wanted to go.

"Let's go *this* way!" Jessaya commanded.

"No! Let's go *this* way!" Bonoi demanded.

However, instead of going anywhere they just went around and around in circles.

Jessaya turned to glare at her cousin. "You sound just like a pixie," she accused. "You want your own way."

"No, *you're* like a pixie. You tuggle all the time," Bonoi argued.

"I wouldn't tuggle if you..." All of a sudden Jessaya stopped arguing. "There's another log," she said happily as she pointed down the river. "Why don't you ride that one?"

"But I found this one," Bonoi grumbled. "You go to the other log. You spotted it."

Jessaya was about to argue back, but as she stared at the second log, she noticed there was an eye on it. "Paddle to shore," she yelled frantically.

"You're not the leader!" Bonoi protested.

"Paddle! It's no time to tuggle!" Jessaya boomed. "That's no log! That's a crocodile!"

Bonoi and Jessaya paddled as fast as they could to shore. They jumped from the log and ran up the banks as they heard the crocodile snap his powerful jaws. The two of them didn't stop running till they were safe beneath the huge, old baobab tree. They tumbled to the ground, panting with relief.

"I'm glad we finally stopped tuggling," Bonoi whispered between breaths. "Aren't you?"

Jessaya nodded, grinning with agreement. Then she pointed to the baobab tree. "Perhaps now we can finish the fort."

"I think we can," Bonoi agreed as he reached out to touch the gnarled trunk. "No tuggling?"

"No tuggling." Jessaya proclaimed as she began to climb the tree.

The two spent the rest of the day in the baobab tree, building the best fort Jessaya had ever seen. Then, as the sun set, she felt her eyes get heavy. "Tomorrow, Bonoi," she said wearily, "please take those rainbow pixies home."

"I told you," Bonoi insisted. "We didn't bring any."

"Are you sure?" Jessaya asked slowly.

"I'm sure." Bonoi nodded.

She took off one sandal and offered it to her cousin. "Then here. Take this home with you tomorrow."

"But why?" Bonoi looked puzzled.

"Because," Jessaya explained, "then you'll have one and I'll have one. And we'll both have a reminder not to tuggle again."

"I don't know if I need a reminder," Bonoi said with a shudder as he reached for the sandal. "After that crocodile, how could I ever forget?"

"Just in case," Jessaya answered as she watched Bonoi tuck the sandal into his belt.

That night, Jessaya went to sleep quickly, happy to have at last made peace with her cousin. However, she knew she still needed to solve the problem of the pixies. So, as she slept, she clutched a sack containing all the small things in the room she could find. The remaining sandal was the only thing she had left on the floor for the rainbow pixies to tuggle over.

She awoke to the voices of the pixies. She stared at them, shimmering in the darkness and sighed. "If only you could stop tuggling, you'd be so beautiful," she murmured as she reached out for her shoe.

"We'll never stop tuggling," the pixies declared.

"Then I'll just have to put my sandal up high, where you can't reach it," she exclaimed as she rose from the bed and placed the sandal on the top shelf above her. "But," she added calmly over the protests of the pixies, "I'll be nice. I'll tell you where the other one is. Bonoi has the matching sandal and if you sneak into his pack tonight…" Jessaya paused to smile. Then she continued, "You can go home with the sandal tomorrow and tuggle all the way there."

In a flash, the rainbow pixies were gone. Jessaya stared into the darkness where their shimmering colors had just been. Then she tumbled into bed, looking forward, at last, to long, peaceful dreams without the pixies.

The Little Caballero

Once upon a time, beneath a sky bright with stars, a young boy rode down a narrow pathway on his pony. He was a lowly stable boy from the Casa de Caballeros, a great hall of famous knights. His name was Pablo. Tonight, however, he called himself Sir Pablo. He clanked along in a suit of armor, much too large for him, hoping to go unnoticed as he searched for the King's army.

Ahead of him, the moon was setting behind the western hills. Against its light, he could see the silhouette of a face, crude and terrifying. It was the face of the stone giant.

For a hundred years, that face had only been a rocky ridgeline above the kingdom as the giant slumbered deeply in an ancient wizard's curse. Tomorrow, though, was the hundredth day of the hundredth year and on that day the giant always woke. He would be awake just until sunset, but in that time he could destroy the whole kingdom. That's why the King and his army were preparing for battle. Pablo wanted to be among them.

All at once, a voice croaked through the darkness, "Who are you out on this wicked night?"

The boy stared through the gloom at an old man on the trail before him. He was dressed in a ragged white tunic and bent over a gnarled wooden cane. "I am the brave caballero, Sir Pablo," Pablo replied with a voice as deep as he could manage.

The old man looked at him with squinting eyes. "Why that's just a pony and you're no bigger than a boy."

"I'm not a boy," Pablo said hastily. "I'm just short."

"Short is fine, if you're smart," the old man said with a wink. Then he shook his head. "Those fools. I tried to warn them. A whole army cannot defeat the giant. I know. I was there."

"You were there? A hundred years ago?"

"I was just a boy," croaked the old man, "but I remember. Nothing could stop that giant. No sharp sword. No swift arrow. Not even burning oil can harm him. He's made of stone."

The boy shook his head. "Something must stop him."

"Not their meager weapons," the man snorted. "I tried to give them this. None would take it, but perhaps you will."

The boy reached down to accept what the old man held in his hand. He studied it in the darkness. "It's only a rope."

"A silken rope," the man corrected. "Strong enough to trip a giant, even one made of stone." The old man laughed. "Tie the rope between two trees where the earth is full of boulders. Lead him there so he will trip and crack against the rocks—"

"Yes! I see!" cried the little caballero. "The giant will crumble into pieces. Ha! That will stop him, won't it?"

"You must be smart. You must trick the giant," warned the old man.

"I will. You'll see," the boy assured him as he turned his pony down the path into the darkness.

However, he had not gone far when another voice called to him, "Who is this, alone on such a terrible night?"

The boy recognized the voice as an old man's. "It is me, Sir Pablo. Don't you remember? You gave me the rope."

"Oh, that silly old rope," cackled the speaker. "You must have been talking to my brother."

Then the boy saw an old man step toward him from the side of the trail. He looked very much like the first, but he had on a dark tunic instead of a white one. "My brother's wrong," he said as his voice cracked with age. "Using trickery won't stop the giant. You must distract him from his angry thoughts."

"Distract him? What with?" Pablo asked slowly.

"With this." The old man held out a leather pouch. "It is a music box from a far-off land. Just turn the key and it will play a wonderful melody. It will distract the giant long enough for him to fall asleep again."

Pablo pulled out the box and turned the key. The melody was extremely beautiful. "No one could resist this song," he said happily. "Yes, this could stop the giant."

104

"Be very, very persuasive, Sir Pablo." warned the old man. "You must convince the giant to listen."

"I will," the boy assured him as he rode on. "I will."

The little caballero had soon left the second man far behind as his pony trotted down the dark trail. It was not long, however, till the brave Sir Pablo came upon yet another man in his path. This man seemed ancient. He was stooped over double as he hobbled along with his cane. His tunic was half white and half dark. He called out to the boy in a weak and weary voice, "Stop a minute. I must speak to you."

Pablo stopped. "I have met your brothers," he said.

"So you have," the old man replied with a great sigh. "And they have given you much advice. I warn you, though, my brothers' plans are mere manipulation. Neither way will work for long. You need a lasting solution to truly stop the giant."

Pablo held out his hand. "I have accepted the rope of silk and the musical box. I will accept your gift too."

The old man shook his head. "I have nothing to give you but wise words—all you need, you carry within."

The boy leaned forward. "What do you mean?"

"I've spent a lifetime thinking about that giant, wondering how to stop an enemy that can't be stopped," the tired old man began. "My brothers have too. They have some clever ideas, but they fail to recognize something very important. They cannot see what every enemy has the potential to become."

The old man closed his eyes for a moment as if he had fallen asleep. The little caballero reached out and shook him. "I want to stop the giant. Remember? You had some wisdom to give me."

The man whispered sleepily, "What a friendly voice you have, my caballero, and a curious mind. Those things should serve you very well. Yes, very well indeed." Then the ancient man sat down by the side of the trail and fell fast asleep.

"Crazy old man," Pablo muttered as his pony trotted on. This time he met no one on the trail, so at the next crossing, Pablo turned onto a wider path and headed toward Granite Meadows. He decided it was there that he should tie the silken rope to trip the giant and end his life for good.

When he reached the meadows, he found the perfect spot to tie the rope. Quickly he pulled the knots tight. Then, smiling with satisfaction he turned to face the eastern hills. He could see the sky was lighter, warning him that the sun would soon rise. "Hurry!" he called to his pony. "We must fly. I must get to the giant before the sun comes up."

So the pony galloped with a heroic heart, carrying his master toward the most dangerous enemy a little caballero could ever face. Closer and closer, the rocky hilltop came as the dawn light grew stronger. Finally they stood beneath the giant, his great head covered with snarls of granite hair. For one brief moment, the boy stared at the monster. Then he tied his pony to a tree and set off to climb the giant's hair.

It was easy to climb. Each granite strand became another step. Slowly, he worked his way higher, squeezing between the stiff hairs. He took care not to break the music box which he had tucked inside his breastplate. Then, just before he reached the giant's ear, the monstrous rock beneath him moved.

Pablo clutched a granite hair, then looked around to see what had happened. Suddenly he realized the giant was sitting up. In an instant, all his confidence left him. It seemed impossible for a mere boy to defeat the power he felt within that massive stone. Just a nod of the giant's head could send him flying to his death.

And yet, when he looked out across the tiny kingdom where he lived, he knew he had no choice. He could see the army of caballeros in the distance. If he failed, they would all be killed—squashed under heavy granite footsteps. Somehow, he had to stop the giant.

Pablo made his way closer to the giant's ear. He wedged himself into a tight spot, then he sat for a moment to collect his thoughts. Finally he called to the giant in his loudest voice, "Good morning, Giant."

"Who said that?" the giant grumbled, turning his head this way and that.

"It is I, Sir Pablo, the bravest caballero in the land."

"Hah!" scoffed the giant. "You're nothing but a pest to me, you tiny thing."

"You wish!" the boy called back. "While you've slept, people have grown. We're much taller now, almost as tall as you."

"Liar! If you were tall, I could see you."

"Not if I were invisible," said the little caballero calmly.

"Invisible?"

"Yes, people have become invisible too. You cannot see me. I'm standing to your right, but you would never know."

"Liar!" the giant roared. Still he reached out with his arm to feel the air.

"I'm not that close. I am no fool. I'm standing way beyond your reach, in those rocky meadows."

The giant turned toward Granite Meadows. He stood up and took a step, a giant's step, that carried him almost halfway there. The motion made the boy dizzy. His suit of armor rattled around him.

"What was that noise?" the giant asked. He looked around suspiciously.

"I dropped an arrow, Giant, but I have more. Or perhaps I should use my sword to shatter you to your death?"

"Your tiny swords are useless against me," the giant warned.

"A tiny sword would be," agreed Pablo. "But my sword is as long as your arm. It will break you into pieces so small you will turn to sand."

Then the giant let out a huge laugh. "Go ahead," he roared. "You cannot stop me. I am cursed by magic. Each broken piece will become another giant. How many giants would you like? Ten? Twenty? A thousand?"

The little caballero panicked at the giant's threat. The thought of a thousand giants terrified him. He knew he must turn the giant away from the rope, so he called, "Giant, can't you tell that I've moved? I'm standing to your right by the lake."

"Some brave caballero," the giant grumbled as he stepped away from the meadow. "Running from me are you? I hear your rattle."

"Running? Oh no! You misunderstand," Pablo protested as his armor clanked with each step of the giant. "We have a custom among caballeros—"

"What custom?" the giant growled.

"Before we battle, we have a ceremony. We listen to this." The little caballero pulled out the music box and turned the key. The beautiful melody filled the air around him. Instantly, the giant stood still, listening to the music. The boy sighed with relief and held the box close to the giant's ear. When it stopped playing, he turned the key quickly and let the music begin again.

Slowly the sun rose in the sky. The giant nodded his head ready to fall asleep. But then, just as Pablo thought the plan would work, the giant became restless. Between songs, the monster announced, "That's enough. I'm ready to battle."

"Just one more time and we'll be through," the boy said, quickly turning the key. As the music played, he searched his mind for some way to trick the giant or distract him. All he could think of, though, were the wise words of the third brother.

"I've got a curious mind and a friendly voice, but what good could that do?" Pablo asked himself. He felt there was a new idea behind those words that he couldn't quite grasp.

"Time to battle," the giant grunted as the music

stopped. He picked up a boulder the size of the royal castle itself.

"I can't battle yet..." the boy called frantically.

"Fight or I'll call you a coward," the giant warned.

"No!" shouted the boy. "Call me Sir Pablo."

"Sir Pablo," snarled the giant. "Sir Pablo, the coward."

The little caballero felt his anger rising. "And what shall I call you?" he taunted. "Bully or Monster or... or..." Suddenly, Pablo smiled, understanding the wisdom of the third brother. "What is your name?" he asked with curiosity. "Do giants have a name?"

The giant was taken by surprise. "Of course they do," he answered proudly. "My name is Stonehead."

"I like that name," Pablo said matter-of-factly.

The giant was silent for a moment, not trusting his invisible enemy. The little caballero used that silence to ask calmly, "Stonehead, I know very little about giants. Could you tell me what they eat?"

"I don't eat, so there's no way for you to starve or poison me."

"No, I wasn't thinking that at all. It's just..." Pablo paused, working to make his voice sound as friendly as possible. "I just wonder what it's like being so strong and made of stone."

"Why do you ask?" Stonehead rumbled.

"Simply because I'm curious," the boy replied.

And so the giant, quite pleased to have someone take an interest in him, began to talk about himself. Pablo listened carefully, with genuine attention. Every so often, he asked questions that would lead the giant deeper into his story. Gradually, the little caballero heard the legend of the wizard and the curse. And eventually, Pablo was able to share the reasons people had feared the giant so.

Then, as a golden sun glinted on the western hills, the boy noticed a massive swarm at the giant's feet. At first Pablo thought it was an army of insects. Soon, he realized it was the army of caballeros, finally come to battle the giant.

Stonehead was annoyed. "Those pesky things, what are they? They look like people."

"They are," Pablo said sheepishly.

"You said people had grown very tall and become invisible."

"I lied," Pablo admitted with regret.

The giant grumbled with disappointment, "You tricked me!"

"I know. I was afraid of you." The little caballero sighed. "Now I see I had no reason to fear you. Please forgive me."

Stonehead thought a moment. Then he grinned. "I will if you show yourself to me."

"Certainly. Just raise your hand to your ear," the boy said.

The giant raised his awesome hand. Pablo clambered onto the rough palm. Carefully, the giant stared at the little speck he held. "You know, don't you, I could drop you to your death?"

"I know," said the little caballero as the giant leaned over and set him on the ground. "Good night

Stonehead," he called.

"Come see me again," the giant rumbled sleepily. Then the giant stepped carefully over the army of caballeros and lay down along the hilltop, closing his eyes with the sunset.

Wearily, Pablo wandered down the hill to find his pony. His heart was filled with sadness. He did not even notice the cries of the caballeros who were still trying to kill the giant with their swords. He climbed on his pony and started home.

Along the way he passed hundreds of people streaming out from their homes. "It's a miracle," he heard them cry. "The giant did nothing. We're all safe." Pablo just smiled and rode on.

Finally, he stopped beside the third brother, still fast asleep beside the trail. Pablo woke him gently.

The ancient man stretched and looked around. Then he grinned at Pablo and asked, "Did you defeat your enemy, little caballero?"

The boy shook his head. He thought about all his intricate plans to destroy and deceive the giant. It was amazing, in the end, how easy it had been to stop him. He put a hand on the old man's shoulder. "Defeat him? No," he answered calmly. "It was so much simpler just to make him my friend."

To Build a Dragon

Once there was a mystical mountain called Tarri-Nin. It was a beautiful place filled with gushing waterfalls and lush green meadows. Throughout its thick pine forests, lived magical beings. Some of them, like the fairies and elves and naiads and nymphs, were filled with joy and laughter. Others—the trolls and goblins and banshees—were of a more somber nature.

There were no humans on Tarri-Nin because it was surrounded by a deep gorge. The only way to reach the mountain was a gap in the gorge called The Gate. No person dared to pass through The Gate for it was guarded by a huge and fearsome dragon.

The dragon's name was Elifore, but his friends called him Eli. He was the most respected creature on the mountain for, without him, Tarri-Nin might be overrun by people and the forest could disappear. That's why many of Eli's friends were very distressed when the dragon came to tell them he was going on a trip.

"But who will guard The Gate?" asked Dinnian, the

113

elf, when he came to Eli's cave to say goodbye.

"You will," Eli assured him with a hiss.

"But I cannot take your place. I cannot roar. I have no fiery breath," Dinnian protested. "You cannot go."

"For over a thousand years, I have kept this mountain safe," Eli roared ferociously. "It is time for someone else to guard the mountain for a while."

And when Dinnian saw the look in Eli's eye, he realized it would not be wise to argue with the dragon.

So Eli packed his treasure, tidied his cave and flew off over the deep gorge of Tarri-Nin. Dinnian waved a reluctant goodbye, knowing he could never fill Eli's shoes. What could he, a tiny green elf, do to keep out the humans?

Yet an elf's mind, ever so quick, is always good at devising some sort of mischief, and Dinnian realized his best weapon against humans would be his skill with trickery. "I must make them believe Eli is still here," he told himself with a nod. He searched the cave and found a large chest filled with silver cloth and silver thread. Then Dinnian set to work, with nimble elfish fingers, sewing himself a dragon.

However, it wasn't long till a troll showed up at Eli's cave. His name was Taab and he stood eight feet tall and was covered with warts and hair. He looked at Dinnian with large bulging eyes and bellowed, "What are you doing here?"

Dinnian glared back. He didn't like Taab and his bully ways. He sat up as tall as he could and announced, "Eli told me to guard The Gate."

"Ha! Ha! Ha!" Taab roared with laughter. "A little thing like you can't guard this mountain. Besides, Eli asked *me* to guard The Gate and I'm prepared to do just that." The ugly troll set down two large rocks and some long pine sticks at the entrance to the cave and made himself comfortable. "Listen to this," he commanded as he began to beat the rocks with his sticks. Then above all the racket of the stones and the sticks, the troll let out a deep and terrible roar.

The roar echoed through the cavern, forcing Dinnian to cover his ears. When at last the rumbles subsided, the elf shook his head angrily. "What is all that for?"

"Don't you know?" the troll growled. "I'm pretending to be a dragon, so no one knows Eli is gone."

"Really? I am too," Dinnian began.

Then all at once, a voice hissed, "Your silly noise won't scare those humans." Suddenly, the cave was illuminated by the bright light of a torch.

The troll and the elf turned to see a lean shadow crouching beneath the light. "Gattie!" Dinnian hollered angrily. "You're sneaking around again." Dinnian didn't like Gattie. The goblin was always playing tricks with fire, and though Dinnian enjoyed mischief, too, he felt the goblin's pranks were too dangerous.

"I'm not sneaking around," Gattie snarled. "Eli told me to guard Tarri-Nin." He waved his torch with a snicker. "And I know just how to do it. Smoke and fire make a dragon, not an angry roar." Then he reached out with his torch toward a stack of brush in the corner of the cave, ready to light it.

115

"Stop!" Dinnian shouted. "We'll choke on the smoke!"

Gattie just sneered back. "Then perhaps you should leave," he suggested.

But before he could set the wood on fire another light illuminated the cavern. Gattie shrunk away from it. "Go away, Rikka!" he spat at the tiny figure before him.

"I shan't. I shan't," chanted the slender, glimmering fairy above him. "Eli left *me* in charge of The Gate. Besides, the humans will learn very quickly there is no dragon behind that smoke if they never see one."

"So, what do you suggest, Rikka?" Dinnian asked reluctantly. He didn't like the smug little fairy either. She always thought too much of herself.

Rikka giggled gaily. "That's easy. A dragon needs wings and I found some beside the waterfall." She opened her hand to show two very small wings in her palm.

"They're too small," Dinnian observed.

"Not for long," Rikka said brightly. Then, with a puff of her magic wand, the tiny wings became two huge lacy ones that looked rather like those of a fairy.

Taab roared with vicious laughter. "Those aren't a dragon's wings."

"But that's all I could find," pouted Rikka. "And they're from a dragonfly."

"Dragonfly or not," Taab growled, "they're no good without a body."

Just then a wail came from the entrance to the cave. Everyone turned to see Shanna, the banshee, standing there in her long black robe. "Yes, a dragon needs a

body," she screeched.

Then she reached into a bundle beside her with her ghostly white hands and pulled out bone after bone. "This," she announced with a banshee wail, "will stop the humans."

"But what is it?" asked Dinnian impatiently. Shanna irritated him with all her moaning and complaining.

Shanna rattled her bones with frustration and pointed to a large skull. "It is the skeleton of a dragon."

"Bones don't make a dragon," Gattie said with a snicker.

"But it is all I have," Shanna whined miserably. "And Eli told me to watch The Gate. What will I do? What will I do?"

"Leave The Gate to *me*," Taab bellowed gruffly. "I can roar like a dragon."

"No, *I* will trick the humans with smoke and flame," Gattie hissed.

Rikka fluttered anxiously above them all shouting, "When they see my wings, they'll turn back. They'll think there is a dragon."

All at once the cavern erupted with the echoes of a loud and furious argument. Dinnian covered his ears and stepped back from the pointing fingers, snarling teeth and stomping feet. As he watched the others getting angrier by the minute, he realized something. Though he didn't like Shanna and Rikka and Taab and Gattie, they were still friends of Eli's. And since Eli was very wise, there must have been some reason he asked all five of them to guard The Gate.

With a shrug and a sigh, Dinnian picked up his needle and thread. Quickly he finished his sewing and then pulled the silver cloth to the front of the cave. Quietly he set to work unrolling it. Then he stood back and looked at the head, the body, the tail and claws sewn from the precious silver cloth.

Suddenly, Shanna was beside him, "What is it?" she wailed.

"It's the body of a dragon," Dinnian declared, "but there's something wrong. It looks so limp."

"Oh!" Shanna screeched. "You need these." Then she stuck the skull beneath the cloth head and began assembling the neck and tail and leg bones as Dinnian draped the silver cloth of the body over them.

In a moment, Rikka was hovering above the silver dragon. She clapped her hands. "That's wonderful!" she cried. "You've made a body for my wings!" With a wave of her little wand, she had them neatly attached to the dragon's shoulders.

At last, Taab and Gattie came to investigate the huge beast. "Very good!" grunted Taab from beneath the head of the dragon. "If I stand inside here, I can roar."

"And if I sit on your shoulders, I can make smoke and flame," Gattie proposed.

"You're not sitting on my shoulders," Taab growled.

"Then we'll take turns inside the dragon," Gattie hissed.

"Yes," Dinnian announced with authority. "There's a head to wag, a tail to move and wings to flutter. We can all do our part."

119

And so it was, when Eli returned, he found another dragon at the mouth of his cave. "What is this?" he rumbled.

The great but delicate wings of the strange dragon moved slowly up and down. Its silver tail flicked dangerously behind it. It roared at Eli and spat out a fiery flame.

Eli reared back on his wings and shouted a warning at the strange dragon, "Get out of my cave!"

Then all at once the other dragon laughed—not one laugh, but many—as a troll, a fairy, a goblin, a banshee and a little green elf tumbled out from the dragon.

"What is this?" Eli thundered with approval. "I see no humans have dared to approach Tarri-Nin while I've been gone."

"None at all," said Dinnian proudly.

The ancient dragon looked at his friends with curiosity. "But who thought of such a fine trick? Was it you Dinnian?"

"No, it wasn't me—or Shanna or Rikka or Taab or Gattie," Dinnian explained. He grinned at the others, remembering how much he had disliked them just a few weeks before. "It was all of us. It takes five good friends to build a dragon..." he told Eli, "five very good friends."

A Dragon's Path to Peace

Step Four:
A Win for Every
Dragon

Every dragon wants to win. No one wants to lose. Yet when dragons argue, tooth and claw, everyone will lose in some way or another. It is possible, however, for all sides to win in a disagreement. That way is called win-win conflict resolution.

There are certain skills to solving conflicts, in a win-win way, that can be taught. They all involve new ways to look at problems and new ways to find answers. However, dragons tend to think the old dragon ways are the wisest ones. Even with the power of their third eye, they can be blind to the fact that past methods of solving problems just don't work.

First, of course, to solve a problem you must find out—what is the problem? You may be surprised how much two dragons can disagree over this. One dragon may think the problem is too much smoke in the cave, while the other may think the cave is just too small. Once you can agree on the problem, you can find an answer. The first step, then, is to identify the problem or the needs of each dragon in the conflict.

Second, is a technique called brainstorming. It can be done with one, but it's better with two or three or more. It is a way to create a storm of ideas from deep within—from that part of every dragon that is connected to the highest magic. This is the step that generates solutions for a problem. It is accomplished by letting each dragon suggest as many ideas as possible, no matter how strange or wild they may seem. It is very important to not argue, at first, about which ideas are best. That will break the brainstorming magic. Later you can go back and look for the solution that allows everyone to win.

Finally, you must actually agree to let each dragon win in some way or other. Even when a good solution is presented to you, you may not want to give in. You may still want the other dragon to suffer. You may still want them **not** to win. However, when you can let go of your hurt and let the outcome be good, not just for yourself, but for the other dragon, that's when the magic of peace begins.

And to find this magic, just read these tales from a dragon....

For Especially Eager Dragons:

1. Read the stories and then create your own dragonstorm with some black and yellow paper and a bunch of friends. Cut out black thunderclouds and yellow lightning bolts. Spread them all around you. Get some old aluminum pie tins to bang together like thunder. Then pick a problem that needs solving (perhaps the unsolved riddle in the story) and ask for five possible solutions. Write every one down. Then ask for five more. Keep writing down ideas until there are no more. Then go back and pick out what seems to be the best solution. And remember, there may be more than one good way to solve the problem.

2. Working with a friend, have each of you write a brief description of:
>   a. someone walking by you've never
>   seen before,
>   b. a picture from a book,
>   c. a conflict or exciting event that you
>   both witnessed in school or the
>   neighborhood.

Compare descriptions. Notice the differences and similarities. Recognize that what you see, hear, feel and think about anything, including a problem, may be very different from someone standing right beside you.

Behind Each Wish

There once was a girl named Atima who lived in a fiery kingdom filled with deep pools of inky-black water and large patches of barren, volcanic land. Her father was a trader and she often traveled with him all over the little kingdom to barter for shiny black beads that peasants made from volcanic glass. Then, twice a year, he would join a caravan to a far off land to trade the glassy beads for necessities such as salt and wool and horses. Atima, however, was never allowed to join him on these longer journeys. She was always told she was too young.

So, instead of preparing for a caravan, Atima found herself, one day, feeling miserable as she fished the inky water of a volcanic pool. Because the soil was so harsh and rocky, there was not enough grazing land for herds of sheep or cattle. And though Atima's family could grow enough crops to feed themselves, there was very little game to hunt except small birds and rodents. So, the people of her kingdom spent much of their time fishing the inky pools of water for the strange creatures that lived within them.

There were plenty of ugly, rough-skinned fish in those dark waters. Many of them were blind. There were also eels and giant water-scorpions which were difficult to catch but quite tasty when cooked. However, this day, as Atima pulled in her line, she was quite startled to see what she had caught on her strong bone hook.

It was a dragon—a green-eyed, black-skinned, horse-size water dragon. Atima had only heard of them in legends. She didn't realize there were still some left.

"Let me go," spat the dragon. "You've hooked me in the nose. I can't get free."

Atima looked at the sharp claws of the dragon. "Get yourself free. Just rip the line with your claws."

"But the hook would still be in my nose and it hurts," whimpered the dragon. "I can't get it out with my claws. They're too long."

Atima didn't trust the green-eyed dragon. "How can I be sure you won't eat me?" she asked carefully.

"Oh, I live on water-scorpions, not people," replied the dragon. He eyed her cautiously, then added, "Besides I'm a wish-dragon, didn't you know? If you help me, I will grant you three wishes."

"Three wishes? What kind?" Atima asked slowly.

"Any type of wish," the dragon assured her. "I am very powerful."

Atima's eyes narrowed as she studied the dragon. She was still unsure about his sharp teeth and long claws. However, she couldn't resist the chance for a wish, so she suddenly reached out and pulled the bone hook from the

creature's leathery nose.

"Ouch!" yelled the dragon. "You shouldn't have tugged so hard." The dragon curled his tongue around his wound to lick it clean. Then he added with a pout, "A dragon's nose is very tender."

"Sorry," Atima answered flatly. Then she looked the dragon in the eye. "Now for my first wish. I want to be fifteen instead of ten."

"Oh… what? Oh… not so fast," the dragon stammered. "My nose still hurts."

"Does a sore nose stop you doing magic?" Atima scoffed. "You can't be very powerful if it does."

"Ah, yes," the dragon agreed as he cleared his throat. "It's just a momentary distraction. Now for your wish." He curled his tongue around his nose one more time and continued thoughtfully, "Yours is a very strange wish. Most people would wish for rubies or emeralds or gold."

Atima shook her head. "I don't need any gold. I just need to be fifteen so I can go on my father's caravan."

"I see," said the wish-dragon. "You must be too young to go."

"So make me fifteen instead." Atima stared at the dragon expectantly.

The wish-dragon cleared his throat again. "Of course before I grant your wish, we must be sure it is the wish you really want. My grandfather, the greatest wish-dragon there ever was, taught me well. He always told me that behind each wish is another wish—the one you truly want."

127

Atima frowned. "But I want to be fifteen."

"No, the problem is you want to go on the caravan," the dragon corrected her.

"And I'm too young," Atima argued.

"But perhaps," the dragon offered, "you just *act* too young. To solve the problem, you must act more mature."

Atima glared at the dragon. "If I were fifteen I would *be* more mature."

The dragon chuckled gently. "And if you were fifteen, you might be more interested in young gentlemen than going on your father's caravan."

"No!" Atima protested. "Never!"

"All right then," the dragon warned, "I will make you fifteen."

He closed his eyes and began to mumble till Atima cried out suddenly, "Wait! Perhaps you're right. Maybe I just need to act more mature."

The dragon sighed and opened his eyes. "Now I must start all over," he complained.

"I'm sorry," Atima apologized. Then she asked hopefully, "That didn't count as a wish, did it?"

"No," the dragon grumbled. "But no more second chances. Now where were we? Yes, the real wish—to act more mature."

And then the dragon explained to her all the ways she could show her father she wasn't too young to go on a caravan—such as talking with confidence and not arguing back and doing her chores without being asked.

"And don't forget to look for ways to be helpful," the wish-dragon advised. "That will convince him for sure." Then the dragon said goodbye and slithered back toward the water.

"Wait!" called Atima anxiously. "You didn't close your eyes and mumble."

"Oh, yes," the dragon muttered impatiently. He shut his eyes and whispered some words under his breath very rapidly. "All done," he announced in a moment. Then without another word he disappeared into the murky water.

However, in less than a week, Atima was back at the pool, calling to the dragon. "Wish-dragon! Wish-dragon! Where are you? I have to make my second wish."

Slowly the dragon rose from the pool. "Oh, it's you. You're back," he groaned.

"My first wish didn't work," Atima explained urgently. "I want to be a boy."

The dragon blinked at her. "A boy? Why a boy?"

Atima sat on the ground and sobbed, "I was so responsible all day and all night and my father was very impressed. He had to admit that I might be old enough to go on a long journey, but he said I wasn't strong enough to help him tie down the packs on the horses day after day. I wish I were a boy. Then I'd be strong enough to go."

"Have you never tied down a pack before?" the dragon asked.

"No, never," Atima admitted sadly.

"I see," said the dragon slowly. "Then we must look behind your wish, like my grandfather said, and find the real wish, mustn't we?"

Atima nodded.

"Can every boy tie down a pack?" the dragon asked calmly.

Atima shook her head. "Not all of them."

"And are there no girls who can tie down a pack?" the dragon asked with an intense stare.

Atima thought for a moment. "Why yes!" she said with excitement. "I've seen girls tie down packs before."

"Then you must learn to do it, too," the dragon concluded.

"But I tried all day yesterday," Atima moaned. "I can't! I'm not strong enough."

"Don't say you can't," the wish-dragon scolded her. "With practice you'll develop strong arms and strong hands."

"I will?" Atima looked hopeful.

"Of course!" the dragon shouted emphatically. "And until then, you must find a way to work with your father, so he can do the part that you can't. You'll still be very helpful to him."

"Yes!" Atima agreed. "Together we could do it so fast."

"So that's that," the wish-dragon said with satisfaction as he turned back toward the water.

"You're forgetting the magic!" Atima called. "You need to do your magic."

"Oh yes, the magic," the dragon muttered. He stared at her and wagged his head from side to side, singing some strange words in a mournful voice. "It is done," he said at last.

Atima shook her head. "That's not the way you

granted my wish before."

"It's not?" the dragon stammered. Then he cleared his throat. "Of course it's not. This is the second wish. It has to be granted differently than the first."

Then, as Atima frowned suspiciously, he dipped back down beneath the black water.

In less than a week, Atima returned to the inky volcanic pool. "Wish-dragon!" she called urgently. "Hurry! Wish-dragon!"

The dragon poked his head above the water. "What do you want?" he grumbled.

"I need to make my last wish," the girl explained impatiently. "But hurry. He's leaving."

The wish-dragon sighed and rose beside her. "What is your wish?"

"I wish for a horse. My father said I could go except he has no horse for me to ride."

"That's easy," the dragon muttered. "Just wish for some gold and buy yourself a horse."

"But there are no spare horses in the kingdom!" Atima cried. "My father can't find one anywhere. That's why they go on the caravan—to bring back more horses."

The dragon stared at her with his shiny green eyes. "I'm sorry, but I think you're out of wishes. First you wished to be fifteen. Then you wished to act older. Then you wished to learn to tie down the pack. That's three."

"No! It's not!" Atima answered furiously. "The first one didn't count. You said so."

The dragon nodded. "I did, but I was wrong. It did count. That's the rules."

131

Atima glared at the dragon as she reached into the pocket of her cloak. Then she stomped her foot and shouted, "You give me my wish or I'll catch you again with my hook." She opened her hand to show the wish-dragon her strong bone hook.

"Oh, please," whimpered the dragon. "I can't get you a horse. All I have is gold and rubies and emeralds."

"But what about your magic?" Atima asked coldly. Then she reached out toward the dragon's nose with her hook.

The dragon whimpered again and swam back into deeper water.

"You don't have any magic, do you?" Atima said. "If you did you wouldn't be afraid of a fishing hook."

The dragon hung his head. "That's true."

"You lied. You're a fraud." Atima denounced him.

"That's true too," the dragon mumbled with a sigh. Then he lifted his eyes and looked at her. "But you have to admit, don't you," he asked hopefully, "that I am very wise?"

"Clever maybe, but not wise," Atima asserted. "If you were wise, you'd get me a horse."

"Let's not give up," the dragon urged, approaching the shore again. "There may still be a way to solve this problem. What is it you really need? You can't walk and there are no horses to ride, so you just need something else to ride."

Suddenly Atima grinned devilishly at the dragon. "Yes! I just need something else to ride."

"What do you mean?" the dragon asked slowly.

132

"I mean," Atima announced with a gleam in her eye, "I just need a *dragon* to ride."

"What dragon?" the dragon stammered.

"This one," Atima said as she touched his nose.

And so it was that Atima went on her caravan to a far off land as she had wished. However, she found it more exciting than she could have ever imagined, for she rode all the way on the back of a black water dragon.

And actually, the dragon found he didn't mind. He had to admit it was quite nice to have a different view of the world than the inky water of a volcanic pool. He was always amazed at the blues and greens and browns of the waters that they crossed. Also, along the way, he made himself very useful by finding solutions for problems that arose. And, at last, when they arrived at their destination, the dragon bought Atima her own horse with a lump of dragon's gold.

"Now I have granted you your third wish," said the dragon happily as he looked at her sitting proudly in the saddle. "You may join any caravan you want to and I am free to roam."

"Free to roam?" Atima shook her head. "Aren't you coming back to your pool?"

"No," the dragon announced. "Now that I'm out in the world I might as well see more of it. I never knew water could be so many different colors."

Atima moaned sadly, "Oh, I'll miss you. You're such a wise and helpful friend."

The dragon raised his head high. "Do you really think I'm wise?"

"Very wise," Atima assured him with a smile. "You'll do fine in the world."

The dragon grinned back. "And so will you. Just look behind those wishes for the real ones."

"I will," Atima promised as she reached up and touched his nose tenderly. "Don't get caught by any hooks, my wish-dragon."

"I won't," the dragon said with a chuckle. Then he turned and headed down the road for a large green pool of sparkling water.

Dragonstorms

Long ago, in the midst of a thick, moist rain forest, a young girl wandered through the tapang trees. The girl was called Chonay and she was searching for fireflies to fill her bamboo lantern. She hadn't gone very far when, in the gloom of the jungle floor, she saw a light glimmering brightly. Thinking it was a firefly, she swooped down on it with a small knotted net of string. However, peering into the net, she found no firefly. Instead, she saw a tiny, lizard-like creature with wings.

Suddenly, the creature spat out a miniature bolt of lightning. "Fly, Thunder," the creature called. "Fly away quick."

Then, with a deep rumble, a second winged lizard flew up through the darkness of the forest canopy and was lost from sight.

"You speak," said Chonay with surprise.

"Yes, I speak." The dark eyes of the creature flashed at her. "And why have you caught me?"

"I was looking for fireflies to light my lantern,"

135

Chonay explained.

"I'm not a firefly, so you must let me go," the creature demanded.

"But what are you?"

"I'm a dragon."

Chonay laughed. "Dragons are huge. You're no bigger than my thumb."

The tiny dragon bristled and shot out a lightning bolt. "Dragons come in many sizes. I am a lightning dragon. I am very important. You must let me go."

Chonay felt sorry for the dragon, but she was proud of herself for capturing such an amazing creature. "Yes," she agreed, "I will let you go. But first I will show you to my father."

She put the dragon into her lantern-like cage and walked quickly toward the bamboo hut she shared with her father. The little dragon protested loudly. Bolt after bolt of tiny lightning shot from his mouth. However the lightning was not hot enough to set him free for none of the bolts even scorched the bamboo.

"What is your name?" Chonay asked curiously as she watched the dragon's lightning fly around the cage.

"Lightning," the dragon declared.

"Do you make the lightning in the sky?" Chonay asked, very impressed.

"Not in the sky," the dragon hissed. "My brother and I create dragonstorms together. I must find him."

"What is a dragonstorm? I've never heard of one." Chonay said as they reached the clearing where her little hut stood. Then, forgetting her question, she called to her

137

father, Lunon, who was standing in the doorway. "Father, look what I've found."

The tiny dragon glared from the bottom of the lantern as the man stared down at him. "Oh!" Lunon said with delight. "It is a lightning dragon."

Chonay looked up at her father, amazed he knew what it was. "How did you know?" she asked.

"They are very rare, but my grandfather saw one long ago," Lunon revealed. "He said they could bring the answers to all one's problems."

Chonay looked at the creature with awe. Then she reached for the little door to the cage. "I promised to let him go."

"Oh, no," her father said firmly. "We must not let him go. He will bring us good luck."

So the tiny dragon was brought inside the hut. Chonay's father hung the lantern in its usual place, on a hook in the ceiling, where it would normally shine the light of fireflies all across the room. He grinned at the dragon happily and then went down the jungle path to brag to his friend about his daughter's fortunate catch.

When the dragon was sure the man had gone, he said to Chonay, "Open the door to the lantern."

Chonay looked at him sadly. "I cannot disobey my father."

"But you promised to let me go!" Lightning shouted angrily.

Chonay hung her head. "I am sorry," she said to the dragon. "My father would punish me if I let you go." And then she left to resume her hunt for fireflies.

When she returned—this time with a lantern filled with fireflies—she found her father pacing up and down the floor of the hut. "What is wrong Father?" she asked him anxiously.

"I should not have talked so much. Because of the dragon, I boasted I could solve any problem," he said to her miserably. "So Honu challenged me to solve three riddles. Of course I said I could. Yet, if I don't, I will owe him a leopard skin. What should I do?"

"Why don't you ask the dragon the riddles?" Chonay suggested. "He seems a clever little thing."

"Speak to a dragon?" Her father looked at her angrily. "Then Honu would really laugh at me."

"No, Father, truly the dragon does speak," Chonay assured him. "His name is Lightning."

Lunon looked at Lightning, skeptically. "If he speaks, then why hasn't he spoken to me?"

The dragon hissed back, "And why have you kept me locked in this cage?" He shot a bolt of lightning at the man.

Chonay's father jumped back. Then he looked fiercely at the tiny creature. "I have some riddles you must solve," he demanded.

"Set me free and I'll solve your riddles," the dragon spat back.

"No. You are my captive so you must do what I say. Solve the riddles," Lunon commanded.

"Perhaps, Father," Chonay interrupted, "if the dragon can solve the riddles, we can set him free."

Lunon nodded. Lightning nodded.

"What are your riddles?" the dragon grumbled.

Chonay's father came closer to the cage. "The first one is this: What can be tall as a tree or small as a flower, can fly like a bee and can change by the hour?"

The dragon listened carefully. Then, suddenly, he filled his bamboo cage with lightning bolts. Chonay and Lunon stood back fearfully. Finally the dragon said, "That was easy. It could be a cloud, but I believe, because of the word hour, the best answer is a shadow."

Lunon looked at him with delight. "Of course," he said, "a shadow changes by the hour—how could I have missed it?"

The lightning dragon stretched his neck proudly. "And the next?" he asked matter-of-factly.

"What can be small as an ant, yet crumble a boulder," replied the man, "can lift up a log and burn but not smolder?"

The little dragon, again, released his tiny lightning bolts inside the bamboo lantern. This time it took longer for the dazzle of sparks to fade.

"A tricky riddle," Lightning admitted, "but I have solved it. The answer is water."

"But," Chonay's father objected, "water cannot burn."

"When it is steam, does it not burn your finger?" the dragon replied.

"And crumble a boulder?" The man shook his head.

"I have been where it is very cold," Lightning advised him. "There, in the cold part of the world, water turns hard. It becomes ice and as it does it grows. Inside the crack of a rock, the cold water splits the stone apart, and over time, the boulder crumbles."

"I see," Lunon mumbled a bit doubtfully. "Are you certain about this hard water?"

"Oh, yes," the dragon assured him.

"Very well then." Chonay's father nodded. "Now solve this one: What is something you hunt, but cannot snare? You might seek it anywhere—in an ocean, a river or a stream, a song, a picture or a dream. And though you feel you hunt in vain, when it's found it seems so plain?"

Lightning looked at Lunon in a puzzled way. "Repeat it more slowly," he requested.

Chonay's father repeated it.

"Goodness," said the little dragon. "This one is not so easy." And though he spent almost an hour flashing lightning bolts around the lantern cage, he did not find the answer. "I will need to sleep on it," the dragon announced at last. "You may tell your friend the first two answers and promise him the third by morning."

So Chonay's father left a second time, and as soon as he had stepped out the door, Lightning turned to Chonay and whispered, "You must let me go. I cannot solve the riddle without my brother. This one is very hard."

"I cannot let you go," Chonay replied as she took down the lantern. "However I can take you, in the lantern, to look for him." And soon they were walking through the rain forest looking for Lightning's brother.

"Thunder!" the little dragon called again and again

141

from his bamboo cage. "Thunder! I need your help!"

"Why is he called Thunder?" Chonay asked with curiosity.

"Because he sounds like thunder," Lightning answered simply.

The girl looked at the dragon thoughtfully. "Is that why you need him—to make the thunder for your lightning?"

"Of course. Together we create a dragonstorm," the dragon replied.

Chonay nodded. "Yes. What is the dragonstorm? You never told me."

The little dragon puffed himself up importantly. "The dragonstorm is the source of great ideas. Whenever we create one, something wonderful happens. Artists, poets, philosophers and emperors—they all need the dragonstorm."

Chonay's eyes grew wide. "Gracious. I didn't know you were so important," she sputtered.

"I am," the lightning dragon affirmed. "So let me free."

"I will," promised Chonay. "This time I will. But first, please solve the riddle."

"I can't without my brother and he's nowhere around," Lightning argued. He spat out several bright bolts filled with frustration.

"Perhaps," Chonay said meekly as she peered at the angry dragon, "*I* could help you create a dragonstorm."

"No," the dragon scoffed. "You couldn't."

Chonay shrugged. "Maybe not. But at least let me

142

try. Tell me how you do it."

The dragon cleared his throat and puffed himself up again. "I send out the lightning and he sends out the rumbles. Each one becomes an idea."

"I see," said Chonay. "But what happens to all the ideas?"

"Then," Lightning proclaimed importantly, "we choose the right one for whatever problem we are solving."

All at once Chonay sat down beside the wide trunk of a tapang tree. "Let's do it," she said boldly.

"Do what?" Lightning muttered.

"Create a dragonstorm," Chonay declared. "Now what was that riddle?" She thought for a moment as she let her fingers trail over a velvety vine climbing up the tapang. Then she repeated slowly, "What is something you hunt, but cannot snare? You might find it anywhere—in an ocean, a river or a stream, a song, a picture or a dream. And though you feel you hunt in vain, when it's found it seems so plain."

Lightning shot out a bolt.

Chonay rumbled like thunder. "Something you hunt—an elephant. No, there's no elephant in an ocean."

"Later! Later!" the little dragon scolded her.

Chonay looked at him blankly.

"First come the ideas," Lightning explained. "Then, later, you sort through them."

Chonay nodded as Lightning flashed again. Chonay let loose another rumble from deep in her throat. "A fish!" she cried.

"A bird!" shouted the dragon as his lightning sparked brilliantly around him.

"A dragon!" Chonay hollered. Then she looked at Lightning and giggled.

The little dragon paid no attention. "Yes! Something magical!" he cried.

"A unicorn," Chonay suggested.

"A jewel," the dragon declared.

"A mountain," Chonay chanted.

"A star."

"The sun."

"The air."

"The wind."

"Moonlight."

"A sweetheart."

"A poem."

"Words."

"The answer—" the dragon began, as lightning flashed around him.

"Do you know the answer?" Chonay interrupted.

The dragon shrugged as his lightning subsided. "No."

"So what do we do?" the girl wondered.

"We go through the ideas one by one," Lightning explained patiently, "till we find the best answer."

One by one Chonay and the dragon sorted through the ideas. "It can't be an animal," Chonay insisted. "Even a magical one can be snared."

"How do you know?" Lightning challenged her.

"Because I caught you, didn't I?" Chonay grinned.

144

"I think it could be the wind."

The dragon snorted. "But the wind is everywhere. How could you not find the wind?"

"A mountain?"

"No, a mountain is not hard to find if you go in the right direction."

Chonay laughed. "A sweetheart can be hard to find."

"But the last line says—when it's found it seems so plain." The dragon shot out a bolt thoughtfully. "Why would a sweetheart seem plain?"

"And a jewel would never be plain. And a star, or the sun or moonlight can be found fairly easily on the right day or night." Chonay shrugged.

"A poem or a word?" Lightening wondered.

"A word could be plain," Chonay agreed.

Lightening shook his head. "No, that's not the best answer."

"That's it!" Chonay blurted out. "The last thing you said was, 'The answer.' It fits!"

"Yes, it might be." Lightning nodded.

"It's hard to find," Chonay mused.

"It could be found anywhere." The dragon beamed. "And when you've found it, it seems so plain," he announced.

Chonay looked at the dragon with a wild grin. "The answer is *an answer*!" she shouted. "It does seem so plain!"

"I'm impressed!" Lightning looked at Chonay with respect. "We created a dragonstorm."

Chonay puffed herself up proudly like the little

145

dragon had done and declared, "We did, didn't we?" Then she reached for the cage door and opened it. "Thank you, Lightning," she said softly with a bow of her head. "I hope you find your brother."

The little dragon flew quickly out of the bamboo lantern. "I hope your father isn't angry," he called as he flew up into the canopy of the rain forest.

"He won't be for long," Chonay called back. "He'll be glad to have the riddle solved." Then she watched quietly as the dragon disappeared into the wide leaves of the rain forest jungle.

Slowly, she made her way back to her hut. When she arrived her father was pacing furiously up and down the room. "What have you done? Where is the dragon?" he shouted.

"We solved the riddle, so I let him go," Chonay explained.

Lunon threw up his hands. "But I need the dragon," he hollered. "Honu was angry about my delay with the third riddle. He gave me a fourth to solve."

Chonay looked at her father patiently. "Tell me, what is the riddle?"

Lunon took in a deep breath and recited, "There is nothing beside it, ever. There is nothing beneath or above it, ever. If nothing is opposite it, what is it?" He shook his head. "It is very hard. I do not know the answer. Do you?"

Chonay smiled. "Not yet. But I know where to find it."

"You can find the lightning dragon?" Her father asked earnestly.

146

"No. The dragon is gone, Father," Chonay replied as Lunon's face fell. She put her hand on his shoulder and added, "But we don't need the dragon. I will teach *you* to find the answer."

"How?" Lunon frowned. "I cannot solve this riddle."

"Yes, you can Father. It is very simple," Chonay explained. "All we need is a dragonstorm."

"A dragonstorm? Where do we get that?" Lunon wondered.

Chonay looked at the little bamboo lantern in her hand and proclaimed proudly, "You and I, Father—we create one."

Three Wise Dragons

Far, far away, across the Dazian Sea, lay a city called Kazar. Glistening clean and bright, it was carved into a limestone cliff above a blue-green bay. Like most harbor cities, Kazar bustled noisily. Its wharves were crowded with ships and piled high with goods. Its streets were lined with taverns and boarding houses for the sailors and traders who ventured there. However, the size of the streets and buildings were three times those of other towns. They had to be, for Kazar was a city of dragons.

In a modest cavern on the edge of the city, lived three dragon brothers—all quite young by dragon standards, and all very talented. Each had their own unique gift. The first brother, Mool, had a perfect memory. There wasn't one thing that he heard or read or saw that was ever forgotten. The second brother, Jat, had perfect concentration. Whatever he began—whether it was a thought or a lesson, a song or a book—nothing could stop him from finishing it. Pozal, the last brother, was filled with ideas. For every problem that arose, he could think of a hundred ways to solve it.

Of course each dragon brother thought his talent was the best and they often argued about it. Nearly every day, their mother had to send them to their separate chambers because they had broken a precious piece of treasure or a delicate limestone column that supported the roof of the cave. She grew increasingly frustrated with their endless quarrels, but nothing she said or did could make them stop.

"What good are memories," Pozal asked Mool one day, "if you have no possibilities for your future?"

"What good are possibilities," Jat interrupted, "if you have no talent for accomplishing them?"

Mool scoffed at both his brothers, "What good are possibilities or accomplishments if no one will remember them?"

And of course, like most every day, the three young brothers got into a terrible argument with smoke and flames and thrashing tails. They smashed a china vase into tiny pieces. They overturned a chest of coins and some tall candlesticks. Soon the whole cave was in disarray. Their mother had a dreadful time breaking up the fight.

"I've had enough," she announced with a dramatic gnashing of teeth. "Until you learn to get along, you can do for yourselves. I won't stay here a moment longer." She took a sack of treasure from under her bed and slithered out through the yawning mouth of the cavern.

And of course, as soon as she left the cave, the young dragons started arguing again. The next day, they

149

were still arguing when a long-nosed, long-tailed, brightly-scaled messenger arrived with a gilded scroll. "Excuse me!" The dragon cleared his throat. "I am looking for three wise dragons. Have I found them?"

"You've found one," said Mool.

Jat sneered at his brother. "Yes, me."

"No, me. I'm as wise as three dragons all at once," Pozal exclaimed with delight.

Mool and Jat snorted in disgust.

Then, with much ceremony, the dragon messenger unrolled his scroll and began to read. "This is a proclamation to announce a contest for three wise dragons to see whom among them is the wisest. If you wish to proceed, nod your heads."

The three dragon brothers were immediately interested. They all nodded their heads.

"Very well." The dragon cleared his throat again. "The contest consists of finding a metal trunk deep within the bay. Whomever finds the trunk first is to be proclaimed wisest of the three and can keep its contents. Do you understand?"

The dragon brothers nodded their heads eagerly.

The messenger cleared his throat for a third time. "I leave you then with these instructions: go two thousand and five dragon steps east, then five thousand and eighty dragon steps north. You will come to a longboat with oars. Then row ten thousand four hundred and thirty nine strokes northeast, turn due south and row four thousand and seven hundred strokes more. Stop exactly on that spot and the trunk will be beneath you. Retrieve it from the bottom and it will be yours."

Then a flame flashed from the messenger's mouth. It caught the edge of the parchment and burnt up the scroll. Jat and Pozal looked in horror at the ashes, knowing Mool was the only one who could remember those instructions.

"Thank you, dear messenger," Mool said with a smirk. "I appreciate your assistance." Then with a satisfied nod at his brothers, he sauntered out of the cave.

"That's not fair!" Jat screamed after his brother. He glared at the messenger. "Why did you do that?"

The messenger shrugged. "The instructions at the end of the message specifically said, 'Destroy immediately upon delivery.'" Then the messenger slithered away.

Jat and Pozal thrashed their tails angrily. Neither could remember the intricate instructions for finding the trunk. They imagined Mool gloating over his victory when he returned with the prize. "He'll be unbearable when he returns," Jat said with a dismal sigh.

"We might as well leave now," Pozal agreed. "Let's go find Mother."

So Pozal and Jat left the cave to search for their mother. They slithered down toward the harbor along the busy streets looking for a sign of her. Instead they found Mool, pacing back and forth on a street corner and muttering to himself, "Was that a true dragon's step? Or was it less? Oh, dragon's blood. There's so much noise. I'll have to start all over."

"Ha!" Jat snickered, recognizing the problem at once. "You can remember the instructions but you can't

151

concentrate on the length of your steps. You'll never be able to count them all accurately! You need my help."

Mool hissed at Jat angrily, "I do not."

"Perhaps, though, it will be my help you'll need in the end," suggested Pozal. "How do you propose raising a trunk from the bottom of the bay? I know at least a hundred ways to do it."

"I'll think of something," Mool insisted as he puffed out a moody wisp of smoke and stared sullenly at his two brothers.

"I doubt it," Pozal replied smugly. "You're as creative as a lump of dirt. I've never seen you do anything. You just read and recite."

Mool gnashed his teeth. Pozal reared back his head. The two dragon brothers rumbled angrily at each other until an elderly Kazarian shouted at them for blocking the way. They moved aside reluctantly. Then Jat lead them down to the harbor so they could continue their argument undisturbed. However by the time they reached the waterfront none of them felt like fighting.

Gloomily, they slithered down to the edge of a dock and stared out across the bay. A ship was being unloaded behind them. They took no notice of the huge chests being lifted from the hold. They didn't even speculate on the type of treasure hidden within them. They could only think of the trunk waiting beneath the water that they would never find.

Finally Jat slapped his tail against the dock and said with authority, "Let me propose, dear brothers, that I am the only one truly capable of completing this task. I am

the one with the perseverance to carry this thing through. Your instructions, Mool are no good without concentration or ideas. And your ideas, Pozal, are no good without instructions or the ability to carry them out. So, why don't you two just give me the instructions and the ideas I need to win?"

Pozal spat a fireball across the water. "Never!"

Mool cracked his tail with a thundering clap. "Never, ever!"

"But then everyone will lose," Jat argued. "What's the sense of that?"

"At least *you* won't win," grumbled Pozal.

There was silence for a moment, as Jat dropped a claw into the water and swirled it slowly, watching the foamy patterns he created. "I guess we'll never know what lies inside the trunk," he said sadly.

"That's fine with me!" Mool smoldered angrily. "I'm sick of that trunk already."

Pozal, however, wrinkled up his brow fretfully. "You're right," he said. "We'll never know what lies inside the trunk." He chewed his lip and tapped his tail nervously as a thousand ideas flooded him. All he could think of were the endless possibilities of what lay inside that metal box on the bottom of the bay. Finally, he put his claws to his head and screamed, "I can't stand it. I've got to know what's inside that trunk."

Jat stared at him hopefully. "What does this mean, Brother?"

"I don't know," Pozal moaned. "It means someone must win."

154

"What if..." Jat tapped his claws together thoughtfully. "What if we all could win? What if we found the trunk together at the same time?"

"That's impossible." Pozal stared at his brother. "How can we trust each other not to cheat?"

"Yes," Mool agreed. "Whoever touched the trunk first could claim to be the winner. I'll never agree to that."

Jat shrugged. "It would be difficult to trust each other, but there is no other way. Unless, my dear Pozal, you can find another solution to the problem."

Pozal stretched his neck proudly. "I can," he declared. "I can solve any problem." Then he closed his eyes and searched his mind for a solution. Finally he announced, "Ah, yes, there is a way we all could win if we could agree to that." Pozal looked at Mool.

"How?" Mool grumbled skeptically. "We can't change the rules."

"We could win in different ways." Pozal explained. "Jat would win the contest. I would win by satisfying my curiosity and finding out what is in the trunk."

Mool shook his head. "That's not good enough for me."

Pozal smiled and coaxed gently, "Mool, isn't there something you'd like from Jat, more than winning the contest?"

Jat turned to Mool with a look of anticipation. Suddenly a gleam filled Mool's eye. "Ah, Jat," he said craftily. "I do remember that glorious ring you found last summer beneath the wharf—the one that sparkled like crystals of blue ice. I might be persuaded to give you those instructions in exchange for that ring."

Jat winced. He chewed a claw anxiously. "What about the fire-glow ring? I could part with that one."

Mool shook his head. "Blue ice or nothing."

Jat sucked in a breath and blew a short flame out. Then he nodded slowly. "Agreed," he said softly.

And so the three dragon brothers finally agreed that Jat would win the contest. Then Mool recited the intricate instructions, over and over, till Jat learned them by heart, while Pozal offered Jat a million suggestions on how to raise the trunk. Slowly and carefully, Jat measured out each dragon step. When he reached the boat, they all clambered inside and Jat took up the oars. At last, just as the sun was setting across the bay, the three dragons stared at a small metal trunk nestled in Jat's wet hands.

Jat looked at it and frowned. "It's much smaller than I thought. I wonder what's inside?"

"Open it," Pozal said earnestly. "I can't wait."

"It must be jewels," Mool said enviously.

"Or perhaps gold," Jat replied with a happy sigh.

Just then Pozal reached out and grabbed the trunk from Jat. "I can't wait a minute longer," he fumed as he pried up the lid with his claws. Then he peered inside the trunk and broke into a fit of laughter. "Mother!" he called out. "It's Mother!"

"What is it?" Jat muttered furiously. He grabbed the trunk back, then stared forlornly at a picture of a dragon painted on a piece of crystal glass.

"It's a picture of Mother!" Mool exclaimed as he looked over Jat's shoulder.

"And it's a very precious prize!" a voice behind them called. Pozal and Mool turned to see their mother swooping down from the sky with her wings spread wide.

Jat looked up at her, then back at the picture in dismay, "That's all I get?" he asked miserably. "I gave up the blue ring."

Mother frowned at him as she settled herself in the boat. "That's not all you get," she reminded him. "You get your mother back."

Jat nodded sadly. He looked as if he could cry.

"Don't look so grim. You had to learn your lesson," his mother said sternly as she took up the oars and headed the boat back to Kazar. Then she softened a bit and added, "Of course, I'm extremely proud of my three dragons for learning the lesson so very well."

"Besides," added Pozal brightly, "you get the distinction of being the wisest dragon. We can never argue about it again."

"Yes, Jat. I'm sure you'll remind us about it everyday," groaned Mool.

Jat smiled. "That's true!" He raised his head high. "That's what I won. Maybe it was worth it after all." He winked at his brothers and added with a very satisfied sigh, "No more argument ever... I'm the wisest of three wise dragons."

Resource Groups in Peace Education

Children's Creative Response to Conflict Program (CCRC). Box 271 Nyack, NY 10960, (914) 353-1796, FAX (914) 358-4924, email: CCRCNYACK@aol.com

Goal is to help children learn to live peacefully with others and to acquire the attitudes and skills necessary for resolving conflict. Frequently works directly with children. Conducts in-service courses and graduate courses. Publishes a newsletter, *Sharing Space*, 3/year. Also distributes: *A Year of SCRC: 35 Experiential Workshops for the Classroom, Starting out Right—Nurturing Young Children as Peacemakers* and *Friendly Classroom for a Small Planet.*

Conflict Resolution Education Network (CREnet), 1726 M St, NW Suite 500, Washington, DC 20036-4502, (202) 466-4764, FAX (202) 466-4769, website: www.crenet.org

National membership organization of conflict resolution educators, trainers, and practitioners. Provides the nation's largest clearinghouse of conflict resolution education materials, *The Fourth R* newsletter, standards of practice, directory of members, *Resource Guide for Selecting Trainers*, curricula, an annual conference, and public policy advocacy.

Jane Addams Peace Association, 777 United Nations Plaza, New York, NY 10017, (212) 682-8830, FAX (212) 286-8211

Named for the first US woman to win the Nobel Peace Prize. Funds the educational programs of the Women's International League for Peace and Freedom. The Jane Addams Children's Book Award is given annually to books that promote peace, social justice, world community and equality of the sexes and races. *Building Peace*, a quarterly newsletter on conflict resolution, targets parents and teachers of children through age 14.

Community Boards, 1540 Market St. Room 490, San Francisco CA 94102, (415) 552-1250, FAX (415) 626-0595

Provides curriculum for its Student Conflict Manager Program (3rd to 12th grade) as well as communication/conflict resolution curriculum for grades K to 12. Operates a Conflict Manager Institute and has a video, *Conflict Managers in Action.*

Peace Education Foundation, 1900 Biscayne Blvd, Miami FL 33132, (305) 576-5075, FAX (305) 576-3106

Produces curriculum in peace education/conflict resolution for preschool to grade 12 through teacher/student handbooks, posters and videos(*Win-Win, Mediation,* and *Fighting Fair*). Runs The Training Institute and provides on-site training. Brochure available.

School Mediation Associates, 134 Standish Rd, Watertown MA 02172, (617) 926-0994, FAX (617) 926-5969, email: SMA@world.std.com

Founded in 1984, SMA has worked with thousands of educators, students (grades 4-12) and parents teaching peer mediation. Richard Cohen, co-founder and director, is author of *Students Resolving Conflict: Peer Mediation in Schools.*

Center for Peace Education, 118-C E. Main St, Carrboro, NC 27510, (919) 929-9821, FAX (919) 929-7465

Peace education programs to foster critical thinking, non-violent communication, creative conflict resolution, team building & multicultural perspectives. Publishes the newsletter, *Peacetalks,* 3/yr. Offers children's services and maintains a speakers bureau.

The Peace Museum, 314 W. Institute Place, 1st Fl, Chicago, IL 60610, (312) 440-1860, FAX (312) 440-1267

Art/history museum committed to exploring creative non-violent solutions to social issues through education, community involvement and exhibitions chronicling efforts to attain peace.

159

Peace Links, 729 8th St. S.E., Suite 300, Washington D.C. 20003, (202) 544-0805, FAX (202) 544-0809, email: peacelinks@igc.apc.org

A national network of over 30,000 concerned citizens committed to education regarding national security issues, cultural diversity, global cooperation, citizen diplomacy, and promoting nonviolent conflict resolution in local communities. Programs include: Pen Pals for Peace, *Connection Newsletter*, Action Kits on several topics including conflict resolution.

Center for Holocaust, Genocide & Peace Studies (Mailstop 402), University of Nevada, Reno, Reno NV 89557 (702) 784-6767, FAX (702) 784-6611

Promotes analysis of the causes of the Holocaust and other episodes of genocide in modern society. Focuses on developing strategies for prevention in the areas of conflict resolution, awareness, critical thinking and tolerance through public programming, research, publications, conferences and courses of study.

Wilmington College Peace Resource Center, Pyle Center Box 1183, Wilmington OH 45177, (937) 382-5338, email: prc@wilmington.edu

Provides a book purchase service and audio-visual rentals nationwide. Subjects include conflict resolution, prejudice/understanding, peacemaking, nonviolence, the atomic bombings, and more. Free catalogs available on request.

Children as the Peacemakers, 1591 Shrader St., San Francisco, CA 94117, (415) 753-0394 FAX (415) 731-3806

Founded to empower children to think constructively about peace and unite with children of other cultures. Programs include: The International Children's Peace Prize, World Peace Missions, The Banner of Hope, the *Making Friends* book and Peace Clubs.